THE THORN OF A ROSE

by

AUGUSTINA VAN HOVEN

ISBN-13: 978-0997715910

Cover design by Leah Kaye Suttle
Edited by Clare Wood, Self-Publishing Services LLC
Formatted by Self-Publishing Services LLC.

www.SelfPublishingServices.com

DEDICATION

For my mother, who always had faith in me. I miss her terribly.

TABLE OF CONTENTS

ACKNOWLEDGMENTS

Thanks to all the members of the Inland Empire Chapter of RWA for their help, support, and critiques.

Chapter 1
It Begins Again

A cemetery is like a train station, with some travelers arriving while others are still waiting to board. A few remain in limbo, unable to go back or move on.

Senator Ashley Halliday hurried through the entrance of Morris Hill Cemetery. She'd parked her car along the street, and that meant a long walk to the burial site. Judging by all the cars parked along the road that wandered through the entire graveyard, it was a good decision. After the service, the traffic would be terrible.

She glanced at her watch; if she took the short cut through the old section of the cemetery, she would save about ten minutes. While the road made a large loop through the graveyard, the shortcut ran almost diagonally through the center. Thank heavens she'd worn her boots. The ground was damp, and the clouds promised more rain.

A short way up, her path was blocked by a clump of thorn bushes, and she was forced to step around an old broken headstone. She couldn't tell what type of stone it was; only that it wasn't marble like those around it. The grave marker had a large crack running down one side and lichen stains covered the surface. The writing was barely legible. It looked sad, the final resting place for a soul long forgotten by friends and loved ones. Something about the stone made her bend down to read the words. She had to rub dirt out of some of the lettering to make out what was there: "John Jacob Leeds 1856–1890. Squandered Potential."

A tear ran down her cheek and landed on the ground. What painful words to describe such a short life. She stood and patted her face with a glove. There wasn't time to linger. The funeral was starting in a few minutes, and she couldn't arrive late. Perhaps she could stop and examine the stone more closely on her way back to the car.

Abaddon wandered along the edges of the crowd. Someone here had been touched by an angel. He could smell it. As he wandered closer, the scent became stronger and more distinctive. Gabriel. He wanted to spit. All his carefully laid plans were constantly upset by that meddler; it was time to return the favor.

A few more steps and he could see her, a spirit clearly given a second chance at life. What was her name? He searched his mind. With so many millennia of memories and plans, it always took a moment to grasp the piece of information he needed. Rose. That was it, Rose Van Buren Leeds.

As he watched her, she took a step closer to the man next to her. Abaddon frowned. He knew that face, Stephen Winship. A growl escaped his lips. So that was what Gabriel had been up to. He grinned. Well then, let us begin our game, king's pawn to king four.

John Leeds sat on the crooked edge of his stone, blinking in the light. He rubbed a dirty hand over his face and stared at the unfamiliar surroundings. Large oak and pine trees shaded the ground. A clump of overgrown thorn bushes stood on his right. The wind came in gusts, and it whipped his long sandy-colored hair around his ears and neck. Something had happened, but he couldn't figure out what it was.

The last thing he remembered before he died was leaving Porter's Saloon with a bottle of whiskey and walking home. He stretched his arms and legs. Every joint and muscle felt stiff. A quick inventory showed his clothes hung in tatters.

To stretch his muscles, John took a few tentative steps but found his movements limited to the confines of his burial plot. He turned in time to see a woman in strange clothes disappearing through the trees. What was going on?

Ashley rubbed a tear from the corner of her eye as the casket was slowly lowered into the ground. The service was very moving. Though she hadn't been close to the man, she still grieved.

The late lieutenant governor, James Battelle, had been a well-liked and respected man. The massive attendance at this graveside ceremony proved that. All the prominent citizens of Boise and most of the elected officials from both state and city governments were in attendance.

Governor Russell Bartlett stood in a strategic spot behind the widow, guaranteeing himself good coverage from the cameras recording the ceremony. There were times when Ashley really hated the media circus that was politics. Seeing the man politicizing this sad event made her nauseated as the coffin continued its careful descent to its final resting place.

Bartlett would need to name a replacement, and the vultures were circling. All of the prospective candidates for the position were here, watching the previous occupant of the office being laid to rest.

The wind blew a strand of hair across her face. She brushed it aside and saw something move at the tree line. She couldn't make out what it was. It looked man-sized but had no human shape, only a dark presence. A shiver ran down her spine, and her hands started to shake. She clasped them together before anyone could notice. Something had just changed; she could feel it in the air.

Another movement caught her attention. Her heart beat faster until she recognized Representative Richard Fowler walking slowly behind the last row of mourners. He stopped and glanced toward the tree line and then turned back to the funeral. His eyes met hers, and the corners of his mouth turned up into a devilish smile completely out of place for this somber event. He nodded his head and continued walking.

Ashley didn't allow any emotion to show on her face. She swallowed. Her instincts had been correct. There was an undercurrent running through the crowd. Richard obviously knew something, and there would be a gathering after the funeral.

The minister concluded his prayer, and people began dispersing; some greeted friends and acquaintances while others offered their condolences to Mrs. Lois Battelle and her children.

Ashley scanned the crowd for Richard and any of his legislative associates. She turned and stepped back with a start. Senator Mike Hampton had walked up while she was distracted and now stood beside her. "Senator Halliday," he said. "The governor would like you to attend a short meeting in his office at ten on Monday morning. We hope you can make it."

Ashley kept her face blank. This man was the governor's personal weasel and under no circumstances to be trusted. She gave a quick smile. "I'll check my calendar to be sure, but I think I can make it."

Hampton gave her his used-car-salesman grin. "That's excellent. I'll tell Governor Bartlett. We'll see you on Monday." He turned and walked over to another senator.

The wind picked up, bringing dark clouds with it. It would probably rain within the hour. She glanced back to the tree line but saw no sign of the person or thing she'd seen before. The thought of it made her shiver again, and she pulled up the fur collar on her coat. Still, that was the direction Richard had taken. She put her hands in her pockets and started walking.

Ashley found what she was looking for at the edge of the oldest part of the cemetery. Richard leaned against a large weathered headstone. In a small circle around him stood Representative Frank Woodward and his wife, Marge, Representative Marion Austin and her husband, Sam, and Representative Stephen Winship, Ashley's ex-fiancé, and his new wife, Rose.

She should have known. This was the same group that had championed the Grocery Tax Relief Act during the last legislative session, earning all of them a place on the governor's most-hated list.

Richard turned as Ashley approached. "Okay then, the gang's all here. I call this conspiratorial meeting to order."

"Richard, really." Marion, a matron with steel-colored hair, shook her head. "I'm glad you're here, Ashley. It's good to see you again."

The others gave nods and waves of greeting. Ashley turned to Stephen. It felt odd to see him. Granted, Ashley had been the one who broke off their engagement, but to have him find someone else and marry her two months later, well it hurt.

"Hey, Ash, thanks for coming," Stephen said.

Richard chuckled. He was always quick to pick up on the undercurrents of any situation. Ashley sighed. "All right Richard, spill." He smiled at her. "It has come to my attention that our beloved governor is planning to cut the school budget during the next legislative session."

"What? Why?" Marion said, looking flustered.

Frank, a large man with a handlebar mustache, scowled. "Are you sure about this?"

Richard nodded. "It comes from a reliable source." He glanced at Stephen.

Stephen raised his eyebrows, and Richard nodded.

Ashley watched this exchange carefully. What was it that Stephen guessed about the source of Richard's information?

Frank cleared his throat. "There is no way he can do that. As soon as the teacher's union gets wind of it, they'll have their people melting the phone lines of every member in the house and senate."

Richard nodded. "That would normally be the case, but this time he's hiding it well."

Marion shook her head. "There is no way you can hide the fact that you are cutting the education budget; somebody will notice."

Richard's face lit up in a devilish grin. "Yes, you can, if you are subscribing to the federal Enhanced Education Plan."

Frank raised his eyebrows. "Why on earth would he want to get the state embroiled in that mess? When he ran for office, he made a big point of supporting local control over schools."

The wind picked up, and Ashley shivered. Stephen slipped his arm around Rose and pulled her closer to him, her honey-colored hair shining against his black coat. Rose looked up at him and smiled.

Ashley closed her eyes. Her heart, already darkened by the somber funeral, sunk a bit lower at the sight of Stephen and Rose. Richard's voice interrupted her thoughts.

"The feds are trying to get as many states as possible to sign on to the program, so they are offering some very sweet grants and other incentives. Bartlett can accept the Enhanced Education Plan with its core education standards, put the new money into the education budget, and redirect the state's tax dollars to one of his pet projects."

Marion's jaw dropped. "Surely he's not that stupid. He'll never get away with it."

Stephen cleared his throat. "Actually, Marion, he can. The program standardizes the curriculum for each grade. If he pushes the state Board of Education to invest in tablets or computers for the students, he can take advantage of special purchasing programs being offered by some of the computer companies and save a considerable amount of money. It's cheaper to buy a tablet that can hold electronic schoolbooks and be updated at any time than to buy hardbound textbooks that need replacing each year. If he promises the union that he will use the savings to increase teachers' salaries, they will support him and use their political influence to help him with the press and the voters. With the right spin, he can take away local control of education and hand it to the feds, and the voters will think he has greatly modernized and improved education."

Frank gave a low whistle. "What can we do to stop this?"

Richard grinned. "That's why I called you all here, to start strategizing." He glanced up at the sky and frowned. "But I think we need to either move this meeting to another location or postpone it; we're all about to get soaked."

The skies had darkened considerably since the end of the funeral service.

Ashley waved her hand. "Before I forget, Hampton invited me to a meeting with Bartlett and several other senators on Monday."

Richard raised his eyebrows. "Are you going?"

Ashley frowned at him. "Well of course I'm going. The old fox is up to something, and I want to know what it is."

Stephen looked at Ashley and nodded. "How about we meet again on Monday night. That way Ashley can tell us about Bartlett's meeting. It might have some bearing on what we're going to do."

"That's a good idea," Frank said. "We need a private meeting place though."

A gust of wind blew past them, making Rose shiver. Stephen hugged her tighter. "We need to get out of here. We can use the conference room of my law office, say six or seven?"

"Make it six, and I'll have my bar send over some food and drinks. I think this will take a while." Richard turned his coat collar up against the wind.

Everyone nodded in agreement.

Frank took his wife's arm. "Come on, Marge. We'd better get moving before it's too windy to use your umbrella. I'll see everyone on Monday."

Marion's husband had already opened their umbrella, and Marion waved to the others as they left.

Stephen let his fingers fall from Rose's shoulder and took her hand. "Call me in the morning, Richard." They walked off hand-in-hand.

This left Ashley and Richard.

"Do you want me to walk you to your car?"

She shook her head. "Thank you, but I parked just over there. I'll see you Monday."

Richard smiled. "Okay, but be careful with Bartlett. And here, take this." He pulled a small portable umbrella out of his pocket and held it out to her.

"No, thanks, I'll be all right."

He grinned at her. "I insist. A beautiful woman should always be protected against the elements." He gave her a short bow and handed her the umbrella.

Ashley laughed. That was one thing about Richard; no matter how she felt, he always knew how to make her laugh.

"Thank you. I'll see you Monday."

He nodded to her and turned away.

Ashley walked among the old tombstones, thinking. Why did it bother her so much to see Stephen with Rose? Granted they were still friends and still worked in politics together, but it stung to see him with his arms around someone else. What hurt even more was the obvious love between the two. In all their time together, she could not remember ever seeing that sparkle in his eyes when he had looked at her. Stephen had obviously found his soul mate. Ashley frowned. All her life she had thought a good marriage was an alliance between two people with common goals. But here in this final resting place for many souls, the first seeds of doubt took root.

The wind whipped up, and large drops of rain fell, breaking the spell. She opened Richard's umbrella and moved as quickly as she could in the direction of her car.

John held up his hands as the rain started. It fell harder, and small trickles of water washed away some of the dirt on his face and hands. Darkness formed in front of him, blocking his view of the cemetery. He crouched against his gravestone as Abaddon's deep raspy voice sounded in his ears. "I have an assignment for you."

Chapter 2
Meetings

Ashley shivered as she walked up to the governor's office. The first day of December, and it was biting cold. The weatherman predicted three inches of snow before midnight. Her shivering wasn't based on the temperature alone. Standing with her hand on the doorknob, she took a deep breath. She'd dressed very carefully for this meeting, wearing her red power suit. When walking into the lion's den, it is a good idea not to look like a gazelle.

Ashley stepped into the outer office and was greeted by the governor's personal secretary. "Senator Halliday, you are expected. The governor is meeting everyone in the conference room, down the hallway, second door to the left."

Ashley nodded and followed the woman's directions. She carefully removed her overcoat, hanging it up on the coatrack just outside the door. She checked her hair in the reflective glass covering a photograph. Taking a deep breath, she opened the door.

Two things struck her as she surveyed the people standing around the room. First, she was the only woman there, and second, every man present voted against the grocery tax bill in the last session.

Bartlett spotted her and called out, "Senator Halliday, we are so happy you could join us." He scanned the rest of the room. "All right, it appears that everyone is now present. Please take a seat around the table, and I'll begin this meeting."

Ashley chose a chair in the middle of the table. Having seen the governor in action many times, she wanted to give the impression of neutrality until she found out what the old snake was up to. It was five minutes until ten, and that annoyed her. She had arrived early, but clearly the others had been here for a while. Hampton had obviously told her to come later for a reason. She settled back in her chair and watched the others take their seats.

She smiled at Senator Leo Albright, an old friend of her father's, who took the seat to her right. But to her discomfort, Hampton claimed the chair on her left. Ashley forced herself to remain calm. Hampton's presence at her side was no accident. Bartlett had a specific reason for including her in this meeting, and whatever it was, Hampton, being his chief hatchet man, would make sure his purpose was carried out.

Bartlett sat down at the end of the table and steepled his fingers. "Jim Battelle was a great man, a loyal lieutenant governor, and a good friend. I will miss his wise advice and political savvy. His shoes are going to be difficult to fill, but that is the task that I have."

Several people around the table shifted their positions. Ashley sat a little straighter.

Bartlett continued. "I want a lieutenant who can handle the senate and help move my programs forward. I'm expecting more problem legislation coming out of the house next term, and I need someone who can deal with that." He paused and looked at the faces around the table. "I have thought about this carefully, and each one of you in this room is on my short list."

Ashley moved quickly along the sidewalk with her head down, trying to keep the wind from blowing in her face. The sky had that particular look it always gets just before the snow starts to fall. Ashley lost track of her surroundings. She kept hearing Bartlett's voice saying everyone in the room was on his short list for the lieutenant governor's position. Her skin tingled as she thought about it. Being appointed to the number two spot now would allow her to run for governor a lot sooner than she had planned. Her heart beat faster with excitement. Governor Ashley Halliday, the first woman governor of the state of Idaho. She shivered with excitement as visions of her inauguration flashed before her eyes.

The rest of Bartlett's words came back to her, "I want a lieutenant who can handle the senate and help move my programs forward. I'm expecting more problem legislation coming out of the house next term, and I need someone who can deal with that."

Problem legislation? Well, that would be Richard's land bill. She quickened her pace. She planned to be the senate sponsor of the bill. She took a deep breath, and the cold air made her cough. What was she willing to sacrifice to achieve her goals? With Bartlett, there would be a price to pay.

Ashley never saw the man coming toward her with an armload of files, and she walked straight into him, scattering papers all over the ground.

"I'm so sorry. Please forgive me." Her cheeks burned. "I was preoccupied." She bent down to help him pick up his papers.

"That's okay. I can manage," the man answered. He looked up and smiled at her.

Ashley had never seen him before. He was quite handsome, with bright-blue eyes and sandy-colored hair worn a bit longer than current fashion, but it suited him. He had a lovely crooked smile that made you want to smile right back.

"By the way, I'm John Leeds, the governor's new aide."

Ashley raised her eyebrows then caught herself. "Ah, pleased to meet you. I'm Senator Ashley Halliday."

He finished picking up the papers, and they both got up. He stood only a few inches taller than Ashley did.

"Well, Senator Halliday, I'm sure I will be seeing you around the capitol. I'm glad to have met you." He gave her that smile again and nodded to her before heading off toward the governor's office.

Ashley grinned as she walked to her car. Yes, she'd definitely be seeing him again.

John watched the enchanting woman walk away. He had to admit, as far as assignments went, this was a very good one. Beautiful women had been his downfall when he was alive, and death hadn't changed that fact. This new time did have its advantages, like women wearing slacks. In his time, showing a bare ankle could have a woman classified as a wanton. The clothes he'd seen on the women in the governor's office would have caused a scandal.

He shifted his pile of files to his other arm and sighed as Ashley turned the corner and disappeared from view. Abaddon wanted him to get close to this woman; well, that would be his pleasure.

Ashley arrived at Stephen's office at half past six. The others were already there. The food had just arrived. Stephen leaned over the table, opening pizza boxes as Richard set out beer and water bottles. Frank sat and shuffled papers. Marion was the first to spot Ashley. "Hey, I'm so glad you could make it. I was beginning to worry that Bartlett was holding you prisoner."

"I had a client meeting that ran late. Bartlett's meeting didn't last that long, at least not for me." She set her purse down on the table.

At Ashley's words, the others looked up. Stephen immediately frowned. "What happened, Ash?"

Damn, that man knew her too well. "Not much." She gave him a short smile. He'd never buy that. Which, of course, he didn't, and he gave her his, "I call bullshit" look. Richard stopped what he was doing and took a step to stand next to Stephen.

"Ashley, what happened at Bartlett's meeting?"

Ashley bit her lip. She might as well tell them; they'd find out from other sources soon enough. "It turned out to be a meeting of the people on his short list for the lieutenant governor's spot." That brought everything in the room to a standstill.

She wasn't sure if she should laugh or be insulted by the looks on all the faces. Stephen recovered first. "Who else was there?"

Ashley ran down the list of the others.

Richard cleared his throat. "Ashley, don't take this the wrong way, but why were you invited? I mean the other senators are Bartlett supporters." He looked her in the eye. "I don't like this, and I don't trust him."

Ashley stared at him, narrowing her eyes. Stephen spoke. "Ash, you need to protect yourself. Even if Bartlett is sincere about this, what will it cost you if you accept?"

That brought her up short. Even though they were no longer engaged, she trusted Stephen's opinion and political insight. "I...ah...I'm not sure." Ashley looked from Stephen to Richard.

12

Richard smiled. "Well, congratulations for surviving your encounter. We'll puzzle out all the ramifications later. For now, why don't we all grab some pizza, nachos, or wings and start brainstorming about the education problem?"

It took a few minutes for everyone to settle down. Richard tapped his fingers on the table. "All right, let's get the ball rolling. Bartlett wants money for his pet projects and apparently is willing to sacrifice anything and everything to get it."

Ashley set down her slice of pizza. "It's more than that, Richard. Education in this state really does need more money, and we need a new revenue source to get it from. I mean we can't increase taxes, not in this economy."

Frank chimed in. "Don't forget we need to maintain local control. A one-size-fits-all education system does nothing but target the lowest common denominator."

Stephen got up from the table and went to the whiteboard. He jotted down the points the others had made.

Marion wiped her mouth with a napkin. "So we really are trying to solve several different problems. Do we want to focus on only one point at a time or everything as a whole?"

Richard mumbled through a mouth full of pizza. "Why don't we use the spaghetti method?"

Marion looked confused. "I'm sorry, the what?"

Everyone laughed.

Richard took a swig of beer to clear his throat. "I mean, let's just throw our ideas against the wall and see what sticks."

Ashley leaned back in her chair and stared at the board. "What we need is another source of revenue."

Marion laughed. "It's too bad the state isn't like ordinary people. I mean if I need more money, I look around for something I can sell."

Frank looked up from his nachos. "What do you propose? That we auction off the capitol building or something?"

Richard set his beer down. "Marion, that's brilliant."

Ashley laughed. "Richard, really, you want to sell off some of the state's assets? First, we can't do that, and second, even if we could, it would be a onetime infusion of cash, and we need a continuing stream of revenue."

Richard got that cocky grin on his face. "Think about it. We are a natural-resource rich state. Why not tap that and sell timber?" "Richard," Ashley shook her head. "How much beer have you had? We already sell timber off the state endowment lands and give the proceeds to the education fund."

Richard waved his hand, dismissing the point. "I know we do that. I sit on the Education Committee. I'm talking about a new source of land."

Stephen raised his eyebrows. "Are you proposing what I think you're proposing?"

Richard grinned and nodded. "Federal land. They own sixty-three percent of the land in the state, and they are piss-poor managers of it. Every major lightning-strike fire we have is on federally controlled land. The state ends up spending millions trying to contain the fires and save the adjoining property while the feds have a policy of let it burn. We could, potentially, have even more money if the lands are properly managed by thinning the heavy fuel loads and avoiding the massive firefighting costs."

Marion shook her head. "We can't just steal federal land."

"No, Marion. It isn't stealing. It is claiming what is rightfully ours to start with." Richard grabbed another slice of pizza.

Marion looked confused again.

Stephen set down his beer. "He's talking about the equal footing law. Every state added to the Union enters under the same rules and rights as the original thirteen colonies. That means the feds can only own land limited to their special needs, such as federal courthouses, post offices, military bases, and national parks. If you look at a map of federally owned lands in all fifty states, you see only scattered dots in the eastern states, but as you get to the plains states and head west, there are vast tracts of land owned by the feds."

Ashley sat up straighter in her chair. "So you are proposing we demand our state's rights and force the federal government to stick to its original agreement?"

Richard held up a chicken wing. "Precisely. We create a new source of education revenue and do exactly the opposite of

Bartlett. Instead of letting the feds take over our local education system, we take back our land and fund our own programs."

Ashley laughed. "I love it. So what is our strategy to get it through the house and the senate?" The mood of the meeting turned festive as they started to plan what steps they needed to take. Ashley watched as Richard explained his plan with his usual wit and charm. He really knew how to make her laugh.

Chapter 3
A Warning

Rose tossed and turned in her sleep. She hadn't dreamt of being in the cemetery since the angel Gabriel had granted her a second chance at life eight months ago, but now she was there and running for her life.

The uneven ground held patches of snow, and she ran among the tombstones, trying not to trip and fall. Something pursued her, but she didn't know who or what it was. The wind whipped up and tugged at her nightgown, causing it to billow out behind her. Her long, honey-colored hair flew wildly around her face, blocking her vision. Her heart pounded, and she couldn't get enough air. A man loomed up in front of her, and she screamed.

Stephen grabbed her, pulling her tight against his chest. "Rose, I'm here. I'm here."

Rose looked up into his eyes and started to cry, clinging to him for protection and support. The wind around them slowed as a bright light engulfed them.

Rose cried harder. "No. Don't take me. Please."

She barely heard Stephen yelling at the light. "You can't have her. You promised her a second chance."

A soothing voice came out of the brightness. "I'm not here to take Rose back. I'm here to warn you both about a danger to you and your friends." The wind stopped, and only the sound of rustling cloth could be heard. "Remember, I told you before that someone was breaking the rules?"

Rose kept her eyes shut, but she nodded against Stephen's chest.

"A change has occurred that will impact very negatively on your political work and your personal lives. There is no easy way to tell you this, but John Leeds has been resurrected."

Rose's knees buckled. Only Stephen's strong arms kept her from falling to the ground. She shook like a leaf as Stephen shouted, "How could you allow that to happen?"

The angel cleared his throat. "There are certain natural rules set in place that I cannot violate no matter how much I want to. But I can bend them from time to time. This is one of those opportunities. Because of the service Rose performed for me, I am able to contact you both again with this warning. I cannot do more at this time. But keep a careful eye on what is happening around you and your allies. John is here for a purpose, and whatever it is, it will be detrimental to you both."

"How will we know who he's talking to? I mean if he's haunting someone, we won't be able to tell. No one knew about Rose until I told Richard." Stephen held Rose tight against his chest.

"Remember, Richard didn't know you were being haunted, but your odd behavior told him something was wrong. You will be able to spot these behaviors in others because you experienced them yourself."

Rose's voice came out in a whisper. "Will I be able to see him, and can he see me?"

"Yes, and so will others. Remember that I said someone is breaking the rules? Now, I must go. Please be careful, and do what you can to stop John. One rule, however, you cannot break. You are not allowed to tell anyone else about John. Things are different now. If you break that rule, then Rose will return to her grave, and I will not be able to bring her back. Remember that. You must not tell anyone what you know."

The light faded around them, and they woke up at the same time, clinging to each other in their four-poster bed. Rose still cried against Stephen's chest, soaking his T-shirt.

It took Stephen over an hour to calm Rose enough to get her downstairs and seated on the couch. He ran his fingers through his hair to tame it and tried to make coffee. The grounds he scattered on the countertop were physical testimony to his own emotional state. John. Here. In this time. How were they supposed to deal with that? Did John know Rose was here? Why hadn't he asked Gabriel that when he had the chance? Stephen ran his fingers through his hair again. How could he possibly protect her from supernatural forces he didn't even understand?

He looked up from the kitchen counter and watched her, still crying softly in the living room. He would do whatever it took to keep her safe. She was his heart and soul; he could not risk losing her. The angel had said that John was also a danger to their friends. He frowned. Did that mean all of them or just one?

Stephen shivered. He remembered John from the visions of her life that Rose had shown him in dreams, a selfish and cruel man. It wasn't hard to guess what type of entity could make use of someone like that. Stephen rubbed his face. He had far more questions than he had answers. Stretching out his fingers, he cracked his knuckles. He hated working in the dark. Time to get some answers and shed a little light on this disaster. But first, he needed to tend to his wife.

He brought her a cup of coffee. "Rose, sweetheart, drink this. It will help."

She rubbed her eyes on her sleeve and smiled up at him. "Thank you."

He ran his fingers over her face and brushed back her hair. "Don't worry, my love. I won't let anything happen to you."

She smiled at him and sniffed. "I'm so afraid. I...I was going to tell you this morning." She sniffed again. "I wanted this to be a happy occasion, but now..." She started to cry again.

"Hey, it's all right." He took the cup from her and set it on the coffee table. He reached out, gathered her in his arms, and stroked her soft hair. "What did you want to tell me?"

She straightened up and looked into his eyes. Tears still welled there and threatened to roll down her pale cheeks. "You're going to be a father."

The words slammed into his chest like a wrecking ball. It took a moment before he remembered to breathe and for his heart to start beating again. "I...ah...you mean...Are you sure?"

She nodded her head. He grabbed her face and kissed her.

Stephen walked into his law office with mixed emotions and suffering from lack of sleep. On the one hand, he felt light-headed, while on the other, a heavy rock rested in his stomach. How could he protect his wife and child? He stopped in the middle of the hallway. His child. He shook his head. What a wonderful miracle. Stephen took a deep breath. He couldn't tell his friends about John, but he could tell them about this. When he reached his office, he shut the door. A few minutes later, he had Richard on the phone.

"Well, congratulations, buddy. That is wonderful. I'm going to be an uncle." Richard's good-natured laugh echoed through the phone. "When is the baby due?"

"It's early yet. We figure it will be sometime in July. Rose has an appointment with an ob-gyn next week. I want to keep this quiet until she's further along, but I had to tell you."

"I'm honored. Hey, have you had a chance to think some more about our meeting last night?"

Stephen heard a car door slam. "Where are you?"

Richard laughed. "On my way into the bar; I have some paperwork to attend to. Why?"

"Do you want to meet for lunch?"

"Sure. Come over here at noon, and I'll buy you lunch to celebrate."

"Thanks, Richard. I'll see you then."

The morning passed slowly, and Stephen had trouble concentrating. He kept reading the file papers in front of him, but the sentences disappeared from his mind as fast as he read them. No matter what he did, the angel's words kept ringing in his ears. What on earth could John Leeds be doing to change politics in this time, and who would he try to corrupt? Stephen was half-tempted to call up Richard's private investigator friend and get him involved.

A thought struck him: What did John look like now? The last time Stephen had seen him was the night John had betrayed Rose. Stephen had wanted to kill him, but because it was only a dream of an event from over a hundred years ago, there was nothing he could have done.

But what about now? Stephen doodled on a notepad as he thought. He did have an advantage. Thanks to Gabriel's warning, he knew John was here. And because of what Rose had shown him of her past, Stephen knew something about the man and his character. It might be possible to narrow the list. Did the entity that resurrected John tell him about Rose and Stephen? That gave him a fright. But surely, if that were the case, Gabriel would have told them. Stephen closed his eyes and said a silent prayer for the safety of Rose and his child.

Time still moved slowly. He called Rose several times to check up on her. When lunch hour rolled around, he rushed out the door. A meal and good conversation was just the distraction he needed right now.

Richard sat at a table rather than his regular barstool. He still had papers scattered all over the surface when Stephen entered.

"Hey, buddy, good timing. I just finished up."

Stephen laughed. "This is the first time I've seen you here without a drink in your hand." He slipped his phone out of his pocket. "I need to get a picture to preserve the moment for posterity."

Richard grinned. "Smart-ass." He gathered the papers and stuffed them in a briefcase.

A waitress came up to the table and set a drink down in front of Richard. He picked it up and saluted Stephen. "I'm afraid the moment has passed."

Stephen shook his head. "My friend, your liver is going to be pickled by the time you are forty." He pulled out a chair and sat down.

The good meal helped Stephen relax somewhat. Gabriel's warning, however, would not leave his thoughts. There was really only one person he wanted to tell, and that was Richard. After all, he knew the true story about Rose. It would be easy for him to believe the news about John. Stephen had the uncomfortable feeling that Richard needed to know exactly what they were up against. He could try to leave hints and let Richard figure things out on his own, but he wouldn't. The risk was too great. He wouldn't do anything that would endanger Rose. Still, he needed to find out about John. Maybe there was a way of getting the ball rolling with a different approach.

Stephen picked up his beer and took a drink. He held out the bottle. "I heard that the governor's daughter has moved back to Boise, and he is putting her on his staff. Have you heard anything?"

Richard stopped eating. "Really? Hmm. I've never met her. Is she anything like him?"

Stephen set down the bottle. "I have no idea. I just don't like the idea of another possible player."

Richard raised an eyebrow. "Getting a bit paranoid, my friend? Is that from pending fatherhood or something else?" He took another bite of his Reuben sandwich.

Stephen didn't say anything, but he stared at his beer bottle.

Richard set down his sandwich. "All right, something is obviously bugging you, and you're not ready to share. That's fine, I won't push, but if you want to find out about the governor's daughter, why don't you give Ashley a call. She was in his office on Monday. Maybe Ashley met her?"

Stephen closed his eyes and wanted to pound his head on the table. He was really off his game. "I'll call her when I get back to work. So what is our first move in reclaiming our federal lands?"

Richard picked up his drink. "Funny you should ask."

Stephen had just reached his office when he dialed Ashley's number. She picked up on the second ring. "Hey, Stephen."

"Ash, this may sound like an odd question, but when you were in the governor's office, did you happen to hear anything about Bartlett's daughter?"

"Yes, he is putting her on his staff. We will get to meet her at the Governor's Ball in January. I did meet another new member of his staff but not at the meeting."

"Ash?"

"Well, I literally ran into the man," she said, giving a short laugh.

Stephen frowned. This was out of character for Ashley. He almost missed her next words.

"It was just after the meeting; he said he was a new aide to Bartlett. Why?"

Stephen heard traffic in the background. She must be in her car. "I'm concerned. We have a new battle with the governor coming up; I just want to make sure I know all the players on his side."

"I wouldn't worry about it. I can point him out at any meeting we attend. Stephen, there's something I have been meaning to ask you. When I showed up at your office and told you about being on the short list for lieutenant governor, you said I had to be careful of what it would cost me if I got the position." She paused for a moment. "Do you really think it would be too great a cost?"

Stephen pulled the phone from his ear and stared at it. Ambition could be a stimulating aphrodisiac and as deadly as poison. "Ash, even if Bartlett was sincere about his offer, it would make you a part of his administration. You'd be asked to do things that are against your principles."

"I could stand up to him if he's going too far. I may be able to persuade him to change some of his ideas and see things from a different perspective."

"Ash, whoever he gives the job to will be a rubber stamp to his plans. He won't offer it to anyone who will stand against him." He heard her sigh and knew she wouldn't let go of this so easily.

"Stephen, I have a meeting to get to, so I need to go. We'll talk about this later."

Yeah, he was sure this would come up again. "Ash, before you go, did you happen to get the name of that new aide?"

"Yes, it was John Leeds."

The bile rose in Stephen's throat.

Chapter 4
Worries

Rose hurried out the door. The brisk feel of the morning air promised more snow by midday. She enjoyed walking from the townhouse to the bus stop along Warm Springs Boulevard. Even in winter, the bare trees mixed in with the evergreens were a beautiful sight. The yards still showed traces of the last snowfall, and there were icy spots along the sidewalk. In another week, everything would be buried in a blanket of fresh snow. Today, the walk wasn't as pleasant. She kept looking over her shoulder expecting to see John walking behind her.

The bus arrived, and she took her usual seat in the back on the left side. As she traveled to her shop near The Grove, Rose liked to look out the window at all the changes Boise had undergone since she worked in her father's dry goods store in the 1800s. The next block took her past the place where the store had been all those years ago. It now held a two-story office building across the street from City Hall. Thoughts of her father brought tears to her eyes. She missed him terribly, but he was at rest now, his sacrifice the reason she now lived. Rose wondered, and not for the first time, what her father had done to give her a second chance at life.

The bus reached her stop, and she stepped out onto the busy street. Christmas was only a couple of weeks away, and people were in full shopping mode. The bell rang on the front door as she opened it. The shop lights were off, but the light from the front window allowed her to make her way to the back. The building's furnace pushed warm air out through the vents, and the shop felt warm and cozy. She smiled. How many mornings had she come down the stairs into her father's cold, dark store and stoked the banked fire in the round stove that stood strategically in center of the building.

These modern times had so many wonderful conveniences, including the shop's backroom. Hot and cold running water came from the faucet above the sink; no trips to the well or to put a pot of water on the stove were required. The stoves in this time were marvels. Whether electric or gas, heat came at the turn of a button instead of a well-built fire. The microwave absolutely fascinated her; in seconds, food came out warm. All these new things were frightening and miraculous all at the same time: automobiles, dishwashers, washing machines, dryers, and especially the vacuum cleaner. In her wildest dreams, she never imagined such marvelous devices. What would her father have thought of all this?

She shivered. Her first husband, John, now walked the streets in this time. How was he coping with all the new things? Did he feel the same awe and fear as she did? Rose shook her head. She didn't want to think about John and what his presence could mean. She ran her hand over her flat stomach. In a few months, she would start to show. A new life, the child she always wanted, a husband who truly loved her. All the things she had wanted and didn't have before. This was her second chance at life, and she planned to make the most of it.

Rose stepped over to the coffee pot and filled it with water and coffee grounds like Stephen had shown her. Clair, her employee, would be in soon, and the first thing she'd want was a hot cup of coffee, especially on a frosty day like today.

Rose and Stephen had discussed at great length what she would do with her days after she was able to stay permanently in this time. He wanted her to stay home, but the townhouse wasn't that large and cleaning wasn't enough to occupy her day. She'd always loved to design and make clothes, so it didn't take long to hit on the idea of a dressmaking and alterations shop. Clair was the widow of one of Stephen's estate clients, a plump woman in her sixties who also loved to sew.

Stephen had purchased two modern sewing machines for the store. Clair loved hers. Rose, however, felt very uncomfortable with the machine and all of its buttons. In the end, Stephen bought her a beautiful, treadle sewing machine. She'd laughed when he called it an antique. In her day, it was the height of technology.

Rose turned on the front lights. The shop's decorations included two window displays advertising their work to the residents of the city, backed by curtains to hide the shop's interior from passersby. The main salon held several full-length mirrors allowing clients to see the fit of their clothes from all angles, some comfortable chairs, and a counter with a cash register. The back room held two private dressing rooms, the sewing machines, and several dressmakers' dummies. Rose and Clair did a good business in fancy wedding gowns and evening dresses, specializing in an "old-fashioned" flair.

Rose laughed. Common clothing from her own time trimmed with ribbon and lace was considered elegant evening wear in this time.

Rose hurried to prepare the shop for the day's work. Clair would be in at any moment, and they had a bridal fitting at nine.

Stephen drove to the cemetery. He wanted to bring his mother her birthday flowers before the snow started later today. All the way there, he reflected on last year and the horrible storm he drove through to keep his promise of putting flowers on her grave every year on her birthday. That fateful day had put so many things in motion. He smiled. In the end, all the occurrences led to meeting Rose and making her his wife.

He drove on the long winding road that ran through the cemetery and parked close to his mother's headstone. Brown grass surrounded the small, marble grave marker. Stephen got out of the car holding a large bouquet of mixed flowers. His mother had always loved bright colors. He brushed away a few stray leaves from the base of the stone and touched her name with his fingers. "Hello, Mom, happy birthday." He set the bouquet down and spread the flowers in front of the stone. He stood up and looked at the cold gray marble. There were so many things he wanted to say to her, so many things he wanted to discuss. That was what he missed most, telling her the things that were bothering him and getting her opinion about what to do.

He smiled. He should tell her the good news first. "You're going to be a grandmother. Rose is due in the summer. If it's a girl, we'll name her Maggie after you. If it's a boy, he'll be Peter, after Rose's dad. I know how you always wanted grandchildren. I wish so much that you could be here to see the baby." He dabbed away some of the moisture gathering at the corner of his eye.

"There is also bad news." The wind swirled the dead leaves on the ground as he told her about John and what his presence could mean. Then he spoke about his greatest fear, losing Rose. By the time he finished speaking, the first snowflakes had landed on the cold headstone. He pulled up the collar of his coat and said his goodbyes.

He drove along the winding road through the cemetery, heading for the exit. He passed the caretaker's office before reaching the gate, and he flashed back to last year. This was the place where he had started his search for Rose. The secretary was not able to help him but recommended the Idaho Historical Society. The thought struck him like a blow to the face. History. Tabitha Kendrick had proved invaluable during his quest to find out about the angel statue and the history of Rose. Perhaps she could help with his current situation. True, he couldn't tell her what was really happening any more than he could tell Richard, but she could tell him more about John Leeds. The only things he knew about the man were from the dreams Rose had shared with him. Because John was wandering around in this time, Stephen needed to know a lot more about him. After all, forewarned is forearmed, as the saying goes. And searching out what happened in the past could give him an idea of why John's spirit had been resurrected in this time. It could be very important to find out how and when John had died. Stephen relaxed behind the wheel. He finally had something resembling a plan. He turned the car onto Vista Avenue, heading for the historical society on Old Penitentiary Road.

"Mr. Winship, I'm delighted to see you again." Tabitha Kendrick, a woman in her late fifties with salt-and-pepper hair, got up from behind a desk. "I do hope you need more historical research done; I so enjoyed doing the last inquiry."

Stephen laughed. "It's good to see you too, Ms. Kendrick, and yes, I have another project. This one is related the other search as well. I would like to find out what happened to John Jacob Leeds after the death of his wife. Did he continue on in politics? I know he never became governor, but did he ever acquire another office? Did he ever marry again or have children? Oh, and when did he die?"

"My goodness, I see you are looking for a complete history. This may take me a while to find out. It's possible that he may have moved from the area, given the unfortunate circumstances surrounding the death of Rose. If that's the case, I may be required to consult with others to get the information you're looking for. Give me your cell number again, and I will contact you when I've found something."

He pulled out a business card and wrote his private cell number on the back.

She took it and smiled at him. "I heard you have gotten married."

"Yes," he gave her a smile. This was dangerous territory. After all, she had done the research that helped him find out about Rose. With the current situation, the last thing he wanted was for anyone to look too closely into his wife's past and how he and she had met. Not that anyone would believe the truth. A small voice in the back of his mind whispered, "Richard did."

That made the hairs on the back of his neck stand up. Had this been a mistake? If Tabitha Kendrick had enough imagination, she could guess the truth; heaven knew she had enough pieces of the puzzle to put it together if she wanted to.

"I got married last June, and oddly enough my wife's name is Rose."

Ms. Kendrick raised an eyebrow. "Really, what a coincidence. Did you give her the rose necklace you bought at the auction?"

He cleared his throat. "Actually, I did. She likes it very much." He glanced at his watch. "I'm sorry but I have to get to an appointment. It's been very nice seeing you again, and I look forward to hearing reports on what you find out. Good day, Ms. Kendrick."

"Goodbye, Mr. Winship. I'll call you when I have something."

Stephen hastily left the room.

Ashley placed her keys in the bowl by the front door. She unbuttoned her coat and laid it over a chair. All day long, she'd run from one job site to another. She had only a few weeks before the legislative session started, and she needed to get as many of her interior design jobs finished as she could before her time was taken up by the senate. Right now, the only thing she wanted to do was go to bed. What a relief to finally sit down. In spite of her expensive boots, her feet hurt. She closed her eyes and leaned back in the chair. There was still work to be done tonight. A quick glance at her organizer brought a wave of guilt. She really should go over her notes and make some final decorating decisions; she just couldn't summon the energy. If she went to bed now, she could get up early and go over things at her favorite coffee shop with a latte and a yogurt parfait. That settled it. She stood up and headed to the bedroom.

John stared out of the full-length mirror at the sleeping figure on the bed. He breathed deeply and drew in energy like Abaddon had taught him. Materializing on the other side of the mirror took a lot of concentration. He wasn't very good at it yet. Oh well, with any luck, he would be getting a lot of practice.

It took a few more minutes, but he finally stepped through the mirror onto the plush carpeting. His own time couldn't compare to the amazing comforts of this one. He wandered into the bathroom. Hot and cold running water in a house was completely unheard of in the 1800s. Of course, he never had to fetch water from the well; his family had plenty of servants for that. These modern lights were also fascinating, to have light with a simple turning of a switch. No gas or fire to deal with, and no soot on the ceiling. He could get used to this.

Some of Ashley's undergarments hung from a hook on the wall. There were no heavy petticoats or corsets; he picked up the strange garment that she wore over her breasts. The cloth was still warm from her touch. He ran his hands through the cups and shook his head. He remembered the day when Boise's best brothel brought in a new girl from France. There were a lot of prominent gentlemen who paid extra for an evening in her company. He thought of her lacy undergarments, but they were not as erotic as this woman's clothes.

There were perfume bottles on the dresser, and he sniffed. Such a tempting scent, it made his body stiffen. John glanced over at the sleeping woman. Abaddon had said he wanted her distracted. A slow smile formed on his lips. He would love to distract her.

Walking to the side of the bed, he knelt and watched her breathe. What a lovely woman. If only he had more time…perhaps next time. John closed his eyes and began to concentrate. It took a moment, but he was able to connect to her dream.

Ashley walked as quickly as she could but didn't seem to get anywhere. She was late for a client meeting and couldn't find the building. No matter where she looked, there was not an office with that address. She couldn't be late; it was so unprofessional, and she could lose a client over it. Suddenly the scene changed, and she was walking along the Boise River. It was spring, and the cotton trees were full of new leaves. This didn't look right; where were the buildings and the bike path that ran along the bank?

A man stepped out from a thick clump of trees, and she froze. It took her a moment to recognize him. John Leeds from the governor's office. She relaxed and watched as he walked toward her.

"Good afternoon, Senator Halliday."

She smiled. "Call me Ashley."

He gave her that boyish, crooked smile.

She looked him over. He was a very handsome man. His clothes seemed a little odd, but he had such a charming smile.

"Can I walk with you? It's such a nice afternoon."

She smiled. "I'd like that." To her surprise, he held out his arm. She slid her hand through it, and they walked along the bank in silence, listening to the water gurgle on the rocks below.

After a while he stopped and turned to her. He reached up and touched a strand of her hair. She wanted to say something about this personal touch, but he disappeared. She looked around and found herself back on the streets of downtown looking for an address.

Damn, he'd used too much energy examining her room. There were several things he'd wanted to say to her. Oh well, the connection had been made. The next time she saw him, she'd remember this dream.

He felt a pull on his body; Abaddon wanted him back in the cemetery.

John grimaced. Maybe next time he could stay longer.

His body slowly dissolved, and he disappeared from the room.

Chapter 5
Deck the Halls

"I want to remove the blinds from the windows and replace them with drapes and some sort of sheers that can be raised or lowered depending on the sun. I want this reception area done in pastel colors instead of these earth tones. You know what I mean Ashley. I want a cheerful waiting room that inspires confidence and gives my patients a peaceful feeling," Dr. Ann Porter said, waving her arm around the room indicating the area she wanted redecorated.

Ashley smiled at her. "Certainly, I understand what you want. I need to snap a few pictures of the room and take some measurements. I'll begin the design work and show you some sketches and fabric samples. I assume you want to replace the sofa and these brown chairs as well?"

"Yes, but with a good durable material that can be waterproofed. This is a pediatric practice after all, and some of my patients have accidents," the doctor said with a giggle. "Also I want to change the play area. It should be a bit bigger, and I need larger storage cubes for the toys."

Ashley gave her a knowing smile. "No problem. Now, Doctor, are there any other things you'd like to see in my design, or can I proceed with these ideas?" Ashley continued making notes on her tablet. The waiting room speaker played "Silent Night," interrupted only by the receptionist's nails clicking on her keyboard.

Dr. Porter glanced around the room and finally nodded. "No, I think those changes will be enough. When can I see the sketches and samples?"

31

Ashley checked her calendar and then looked up. "I can have them done by December twentieth. Does that work for you, or do you want to wait until after the holidays?"

"Can we meet early in the morning on the twentieth? My husband and I are leaving on the twenty-second for a trip to New Zealand. I'll be back in the office on January twelfth."

"New Zealand! That sounds wonderful."

The doctor laughed. "It's my husband's idea. I have a terrible time getting Walter to take time off and travel. He's so busy. Well, you know; your dad is a defense attorney, too. But Walter is a huge Tolkien fan. He loves *The Lord of the Rings* and *The Hobbit*. I got him to take time off over the holidays, but only if he could tour the places where they filmed the movies. They seem to have quite a tour package set up for that. The tour takes you all over the area. It even includes kayaking. I'm not that big of a fan, but I'm actually looking forward to the trip."

Ashley smiled. "That sounds like great fun. You'll have to tell me about it when you return. Well, I'd better get busy taking the pictures and measurements. I want to be out of here before your first appointment arrives. Thank you for your business, and I'll see you on the twentieth. Same time as today?"

The doctor nodded. "Thank you, Ashley. I look forward to seeing your designs."

The doctor held out her hand, and Ashley shook it. Fifteen minutes later, she was outside in a light, falling snow, heading to her car.

She started her engine to let it run for a few minutes and warm up. This gave her a few minutes to check her phone for messages. There were three texts from suppliers, but only one missed call, and that was from her mother.

Ashley stared at the phone for a moment. Her mom probably wanted to discuss what to serve at the family Christmas dinner. She checked her watch. There was enough time to call her back before she headed to her next appointment.

"Hi, Mom, I got your message."

"Oh, Ashley, I'm so glad you called back so quickly. I wanted to give you plenty of notice that your Dad and I are going to Hawaii this year for Christmas."

"What?" Ashley shifted her position on the car seat. "What do you mean you're going to Hawaii? What about Christmas dinner?"

"Well, I called your brother Bill to check and see what he and his family wanted, and he told me they are going to Disney World with his in-laws. They are meeting his wife's sister and her family there, too. You know his father-in-law hasn't been feeling well, and they wanted a special family Christmas to remember in case something happens."

Ashley switched on the car heater. "Okay, what about Tom and his family?"

"Tom's wife wanted to go skiing this year in Sun Valley. They have some friends who want to go as well, and they asked Dad if they could use our house up there. Dad said yes."

Ashley frowned. "So since both of your sons won't be there, that only leaves me." That stung. She always felt like the least successful of the three children. If she got the lieutenant governor's position, maybe her parents would respect her more.

"Oh, Ashley, Dad and I figured you have so many friends, you'd probably like to do something with one of them rather than always come to our house. You'll probably have a wonderful time."

Ashley took a deep breath. When her mother was on a roll, she wouldn't be able to get a word in edgewise.

"We're going to Hawaii with the Turners. You know Louise's family has a condo on Maui, and none of her other family members was using it this year, so they invited us to go with them. It's right on the beach and has four bedrooms, three bathrooms, and a large kitchen and dining room. You can walk off the patio onto the sand and head for the water. I'm so looking forward to it. It will be nice to get out of the snow and cold for a while."

"I'm sure you and Dad will have a great time, but what about gifts? Do you want to open presents early?"

"Well, because the grandchildren are off on their different trips, Dad and I decided to give money this year instead of presents. You can stop by the house for your check, or I can mail it to you. Dad and I are leaving early Saturday, so if you want to stop by, you'll need to do it Thursday night. We are going to the office Christmas party on Wednesday."

"I already have plans for Thursday night."

"See what I mean, you're always busy with work or politics or your friends. You'll be fine for Christmas."

Ashley raised one eyebrow. It sounded like her mom was trying to convince herself more than her daughter. "I'll be fine, Mom. You and Dad have a great time. I'll stop by after you get back to give you your gift. I have to get going. I have another client appointment today." She brushed a tear from her cheek.

"All right, dear. Have a Merry Christmas and Happy New Year. Dad and I will see you when we get back after the holidays. Bye."

"Bye, Mom." Ashley hung up the phone and looked around the busy street. Everywhere she could see people carrying Christmas packages. People were happily shopping with their families, and she was going to spend the holidays alone in her apartment. She didn't even have a cat for company. Most of her friends already had plans for Christmas with family. The last thing she wanted to do was be a fifth wheel at someone's house. Maybe she could binge watch a television series or something.

Her phone rang. For a moment she hoped it was her mother calling back to say she had changed her mind. A number flashed on the phone, but it wasn't one she recognized. It might be a potential new client. "Hello."

"Hello, Senator Halliday, this is John Leeds from the governor's office."

Ashley raised her eyebrows and then blushed. How odd to have him call after she dreamed of him last night.

"Yes, Mr. Leeds, it's nice to speak to you again." She smiled, remembering the handsome man she'd nearly bowled over on her way back from the governor's office.

"The governor asked me to call you and make sure you received his personal invitation to the Governor's Ball. I mailed it out yesterday with a personal note enclosed, so you should receive it in today's mail."

Ashley smiled. If Bartlett wanted her to be at the ball, then her chances of becoming lieutenant governor were very good. "I haven't checked my mail yet, but I will look for it. So the governor would like all the candidates for lieutenant governor to be present at the event?" She might as well do some fishing for information.

"Yes, he would like that, but he wants to ensure the presence of specific candidates and has sent them personal notes."

This sounded extremely encouraging. "Tell the governor that I look forward to attending." As an afterthought, she asked, "Will you be attending?"

"Yes. Mason Radnor, the chief of staff, will be at the governor's side for the evening, so I'll be free to enjoy the event rather than work it."

Ashley laughed. "You will enjoy it. The hors d'oeuvres are delicious, and there is great music for dancing."

"Senator Halliday, would it be improper for the governor's aide to dance with a senator?"

Ashley really laughed. "I'd love to dance with you, and no, it's not improper. This is a party, and it's not the 1800s."

John made a small choking noise. "Good. I'll let the governor know that you are coming, and I'll hold you to that promise of a dance. Have a happy holiday season. Goodbye."

"Goodbye, Mr. Leeds."

Ashley clicked off the phone. At least she had something to look forward to, even if Christmas was going to be a bust. She checked her watch and sat bolt upright. She had to get moving or be late to her next appointment.

John carefully placed the phone in its cradle and marveled at this amazing machine. How handy this would have been during his time. Instead of jumping on his horse or sending a servant, all he would have had to do was pick up this device and punch in a few numbers to reach the person he wanted to talk to.

He felt a movement behind him and shivered. "Did I do as you wanted, sir?"

A voice spoke in his mind. "Yes, you did well. As the time of the ball gets closer, I will give you other instructions. Now it is time to return to your place."

John hated being trapped in the cemetery; there was nothing to do but pace the small plot that contained his body. He liked being around people and especially working in politics. Walking around the capitol building and working on the governor's projects made it seem like he was still alive. "Are you sure there isn't anything else for me to do?"

Abaddon laughed, a truly frightening sound. "Yes, I'm sure, time to go."

The squeezing started, and he grabbed his stomach, concentrating hard to quell the nausea. A moment later, he was on his knees leaning heavily against his broken headstone, panting. It took a few minutes for the dizziness to subside. The passage from spirit to flesh and back again was not a pleasant experience.

John looked around for Abaddon and didn't sense him. That made him feel better. He was very grateful for this opportunity, but dealing with this creature gave him the creeps. He couldn't actually see it; he guessed there wasn't really anything for him to see. He only sensed shadows and darkness, not an actual presence, more like the lack of one, a dark hole where something should be. The wind blew snow around him. This was the part he hated the most. Standing here with life all around him and not being able to interact with it, no feeling of the wind on his face, no sense of cold or warmth, only the emptiness of watching and hearing but not participating. If only he could sleep, then at least he might be able to dream.

Papers and file folders covered the desk while Stephen sat staring at a picture on his wall, a running stream in a serene wooded area with a deer drinking water and a bird flying between trees. He stared at the painting, but its peaceful setting didn't help. His mind kept going back to Rose and the presence of John in this time. How could he protect Rose from angels and demons and whatever else was out there? He had no clue about why all of this was happening and what these beings wanted, much less why they had involved him. Still, they had brought Rose into his life, and he would not let her go, no matter what. Perhaps he'd get a call today from Tabitha with news about John.

He sighed. Right now, however, he needed to work but simply couldn't concentrate. This time of year, many of his clients wanted to go over their estate plans and make changes. The stack of files on the desk stood testimony to all the work he had to do, but John Leeds kept haunting his thoughts.

Amanda's voice over the intercom startled him. "Stephen, Richard Fowler is here to see you."

"Thanks, Amanda, send him in." Stephen hurriedly stuffed papers into files and tried to clear off his desk. Thank goodness for Richard. He might not be able to discuss what was troubling him, but Richard always found a way to make him laugh, and he really needed that right now.

The door opened, revealing his friend. "Did I catch you at a bad time?" Richard asked.

Stephen smiled. "No, your timing is great. I really need a break. So, what's up?"

Richard plopped down in one of the guest chairs. "I've been thinking about our plans, and we need to get more information on what Bartlett is doing. How would you feel if I employed Jason Tomblin and his firm again?"

Stephen sat up straighter in his chair. "I wasn't very thrilled to find out you had me followed by a private eye last spring."

Richard picked up a pen from the desk and twirled it through his fingers. "Well, I wasn't too happy about having to do it, but it proved to be invaluable in the end. The stakes are much higher this time. You're going to be announcing your candidacy for the governor's office this spring, and the federal land bill is going to need a lot of shepherding to get it through both houses with enough support to override Bartlett's veto. You stung him pretty badly with the grocery tax bill last session, and he will be coming loaded for bear this year. We need to be prepared."

Stephen ran his fingers through his hair. "I've been working with Mandy Sawyer on getting the campaign set up, and I hope to announce on January thirteenth."

Richard sat up in his chair. "Wow, you're going to announce on the third day of the session. That's ballsy. Bartlett will have a cow. I want a front-row seat for that show."

"Yeah, Mandy thought it would be good to announce soon after Bartlett delivers his state of the state speech. I can really contrast what I'm planning and what he has done. I might as well come out swinging. This is not going to be a featherweight contest."

Richard chuckled. "I never thought it would be. This is going to be a busy year for you: a difficult session, a gubernatorial primary, and you're going to be a dad. What do you plan to do for an encore?"

"I was thinking of world peace."

Richard laughed. "I'd settle for peace in this state. Seriously, how do you plan to handle everything?"

"I haven't a clue. I am going to rely heavily on Mandy to handle all the campaign issues. I'll just show up when she tells me to. The session, well, I'll have to play it by ear. Besides, you're the one with the controversial bill this session, and I get to be your wing man this time around." He leaned back in his chair.

"And what about being a father. Are you ready for that?"

Stephen ran his fingers through his hair. "I don't think one is every truly ready for that. All I can do is my best and pray that it will be good enough."

Richard leaned forward. "My friend, I know you will move heaven and earth to give your child the best of everything. Now let me be of some assistance. Your campaign and the land bill are going to need a lot of good information to navigate the many minefields they need to be walked through. Because both will have a lot of opposition from the same sources, let me handle the opposition research. I'll let Mandy know what I find out.

"Well, I better get going; there's a big party scheduled at the bar tonight, and I need to be there to make sure everything runs smoothly. Tell your lovely wife hello for me, and we'll plan strategy later." Richard stood up and gave a slight bow before exiting the room.

Stephen smiled as some of the tension left his shoulders.

Chapter 6
Getting the Ball Rolling

Richard parked his BMW in a secluded parking space at the back of a large house on the edge of the business district. Once the very fashionable home of a wealthy banker, the house had undergone renovations in the eighties. It now held separate office suites for two lawyers, a financial planner, and Confidential Investigations. Located in the basement with its own separate entrance, the private investigations firm offered discretion and privacy to its clients. Richard got out of his car and hurried to the door. The snow was falling harder, and wet flakes collected in his thick, brown hair.

He walked through the door and stomped his boots on the entry rug. Richard looked up to see the receptionist frowning at him.

"Hello, Lori. Is he in?" He gave her a grin.

"Good afternoon, Mr. Fowler. I'll tell him you're here." She typed something on her keyboard.

Richard removed his heavy coat, scarf, and gloves. Footsteps sounded down the hall, and a man came into the room.

"Richard, it's good to see you. Come on back." He pointed down the hall he'd just come from.

"Thanks, Jason. How's the family?"

"My family is fine. Jeannie is busy Christmas shopping, and the kids are looking forward to getting out of school for the holidays. How about you? Are you heading to your sister's?"

The men made small talk until they entered Jason's office and closed the door.

"Have a seat." Jason pointed to the two seats in front of his desk. He sat down, and Richard settled himself in one chair, depositing his coat and things on the other.

"I'm not sure what I'm doing for Christmas, but I do have some work for you," Richard replied.

Jason laughed, as he pulled out a notepad and grabbed a pen from a jar, setting it on the desk. "So what are you going to be up to this legislative session?"

Richard gave Jason a grin. "We intend to boot the federal government off of Idaho land."

Jason whistled. "You don't do things halfway do you? What brought this on?"

"Bartlett, who else? He's got this scheme to fund his pet projects by rerouting the government grants from the federal Enhanced Education Plan to the general fund and using the savings from the new computer textbook program to pay for the plan and salary increases for teachers. The problem with this is local control of education goes out the window. The feds can dictate everything from curriculum, to class size, to testing requirements.

"We all know it won't stop there. Eventually, they will tell us who we can and cannot hire and what to pay them, what snacks are allowed in school vending machines, what food we have to put in the nutrition program, and how to design and build the school buildings. He may catch crap for it, but he will be long out of office by the time all of it gets implemented, and there will be no way to opt out.

"The best way to stop the plan is to kill it before it starts. And that, my friend, is where you come in...again."

He grinned at Jason.

"Okay, what do you want me to do?" Jason picked up his pen and leaned forward.

"First, we need to get information on Bartlett. Find out if he is meeting with any new people. Keep an eye on Mason Radnor; whatever Bartlett is up to, Radnor will be his hatchet man. I am going to need to hire a company to do data mining. Do you know anyone who can be trusted?"

A knock on the door interrupted the conversation. Jason's receptionist brought in a tray containing a carafe of coffee with cups, cream, and sugar. She smiled at Richard and set the tray down on one side of the desk. "Is there anything else you need?"

"No, this will be fine. Thanks, Lori."

She gave him a nod and left the room, closing the door behind her.

"Help yourself, Richard." Jason said as he stood up and grabbed a cup.

Richard got up and took the cup handed to him. Jason poured the coffee and Richard reached for the sugar. After a few minutes both men were seated again, sipping their drinks.

"Data mining, huh? How much and what kind?"

Richard set his cup on the desk. "I need a search of all the state's documents pertaining to any land controlled by the federal government. I want to know what the land has been used for, when it went into service, and if there have been any fires. I am particularly interested in the fire history. I'm trying to build the case on what piss-poor managers the feds have been. I want to know how much fuel load has been allowed to build up, and whether any fire prevention has been done. If a section has burned, then what was the cause of the fire? How many acres were burned? Did the feds do any fire suppression? Were any Idaho lands or private property threatened or also burned? Did the state incur any firefighting costs? Could the fire have been prevented with better management? Things along this line." He picked up his cup of coffee while Jason scribbled on his notepad.

After a few minutes, Jason looked up. "I see where you are going with this."

Richard nodded. "The only way to get a bill passed on this issue is to have so much evidence and hard facts that the weight of the paperwork breaks the backs of the opposition."

"Okay, I know a company. I have used them on occasion for other clients. You'll like the owner. He thinks like you, and his brother is about to join you in the house." Jason set his pen down and grabbed his coffee.

Richard raised an eyebrow. "Really, who is it?"

"Paul Miller, the new guy from district nine. Sam Miller owns Theorem Data Technology. They specialize in organizing, analyzing, sorting, and retrieving data for different types of research companies all over the United States. They are very good and very discrete. All of their work is sent encrypted, and only someone with the encryption code can open it. They get used a lot by companies trying to stop the National Security Agency from capturing information sent over the internet or phone lines. This way, the federal government won't know what you are up to and neither will Bartlett until you make your public announcement. They also won't be able to find out what information you have until you are ready to use it. I'm sure that meets your criteria." Jason drained his cup and poured himself another one.

Richard smiled. "They sound perfect. How well do you know Paul Miller? Do you think he would be a good addition to our team in the house?"

"I've known him and his brother for several years. I think you and he will get along great. Politically, you two are very close. If he doesn't work out as a member of your team, he will certainly be an ally." He picked up his pen again. "How soon do you want me to start?"

"Tomorrow." Richard leaned over and pulled his checkbook out of his coat pocket. "We will be introducing the legislation as early in the session as possible, so that doesn't leave us much time. Bartlett is keeping this well under wraps. We only found out by accident, thanks to you, or we would have been caught completely flat-footed."

Richard slipped the pen out of his leather checkbook holder and wrote while he continued speaking. "Also, Stephen Winship is announcing his candidacy for governor on the third day of the session. I want to help his campaign with opposition research, but I don't want it to show up on any of his sunshine reports. Would this data-mining company mind handling more research under the same account and billing it to me under the lands bill research?"

"I don't see why not. Their client's confidentiality is part of their package. What they research and for whom is not disclosed to anyone. When you sign the contract, you are assigned a client code, and any information you give them or they give you runs through that code. Their employees are very carefully screened and sign some serious nondisclosure contracts. I have trusted them to run some very sensitive data for me; you know that if there were any leaks of what I do, my clients would all bolt. Sam will be in town on Friday. I can arrange a meeting here, and you two can discuss what you need and get the paperwork taken care of." He made some more notes on his pad.

Richard tore the check out and laid it on the desk. "Sounds great. Let me know the time of the meeting, and I'll be here. I'd also like to meet his brother as soon as possible. If he's inclined like us and new to the legislature, then I want to get him up to speed as soon as possible. He stood up. "Jason, I want you to start up the surveillance on Stephen again, and include his wife this time. I don't trust Bartlett as far as I can spit, and I wouldn't be surprised if he tries to stage something to discredit Stephen and take him out of the race. God knows the man can't beat him on a fair playing field, and, given what he tried to do on the grocery tax bill, well, I wouldn't put anything past him or Radnor."

Richard picked up his coat and slipped it on. "Jason, have someone watch Ashley Halliday as well. Bartlett is dangling the short list for the lieutenant governor's position in front of her, and she wants it badly. I wouldn't put it past him to use Ashley against Stephen. I mean, he's completely enamored with his wife, but Ashley is a good friend, and I know he doesn't want anything bad to happen to her. Blackmail is not outside the realm of possibility for Bartlett."

He buttoned up his coat and put on his scarf and gloves. "I'll see you on Friday, then. Thanks, Jason, and as usual report anything odd to me immediately. Merry Christmas." He nodded his head and left the room.

Ashley sat at the traffic light taking advantage of the stop to shift some of the precariously balanced sample books to the floor of the car before they fell there on their own. All during her last client meeting, she kept thinking of the Governor's Ball and the possibility of being the next lieutenant governor. She needed to make a good impression on all the people present. You could never tell when something you said, did, or wore would positively or negatively affect the outcome of an event. Her father had taught her that about preparing for court. He'd once lost a case because the defendant said something stupid that the judge overheard. He also had one complete loser of a client get a very light sentence because he cleaned up well in a suit and tie.

As much as she liked how her special-event dresses fit, most of them were designed to show off her excellent figure and attract attention. That was not the image she wanted to present to the public as the next lieutenant governor of Idaho. No, the ball would require a new dress, something classy and elegant. Something unique that emphasized her femininity but also inspired confidence in her ability to handle the job.

She remembered the very beautiful gown a friend of hers had worn to a wedding in October. The gown was custom-made and designed by Rose Winship. Ashley swallowed. It came down to how badly she wanted to make a good impression versus how badly she wanted to avoid Rose. The woman was always nice to her when they met in public, but this would be a more personal contact.

The light changed, and traffic began to move. Rose's shop wasn't far from Stephen's office. She bit her lip. Should she try to get a dress there or order a designer dress through one of the other ladies' shops in Boise? Stephen had warned her about Bartlett and the job; maybe he would see that she knew what she was doing if she extended an olive branch to his wife. She made up her mind; Rose could design her dress for the ball. She checked the traffic around her and changed lanes, heading toward downtown.

Ashley walked up to the shop and looked at the display window. Two mannequins stood in casual poses; one wore a very beautiful wedding dress and the other a unique evening dress that had a hint of another time about it. Both dresses really appealed to Ashley's taste.

She cautiously entered the shop. The room looked like a typical bridal shop with sample dresses and a raised platform surrounded by mirrors.

A plump, matronly woman came around the corner from the backroom and smiled at her. "May I help you?"

"Yes, I'm Ashley Halliday. I work with Stephen Winship in politics. A friend of mine recommended his wife's shop, and I would like to get a ball gown made for the Governor's Ball. Is there enough time to have that done?"

"I think so. I'm Clair Timmons; I work with Rose. She's finishing up a fitting right now. I can get you started until she's free. Do you have an idea of what you'd like, or do you want Rose to improvise?"

Ashley smiled. *In for a penny, in for a pound.* "I'd like to see what Rose can come up with. How do we begin?"

"This way." Clair led her through a door. It opened into a hall with two rooms. Ashley could hear voices coming from the room at the far end. Clair led her through the closest door. It was a nice fitting room about the size of a small child's bedroom. The room contained a three-sided mirror surrounding a small raised platform, two comfortable chairs separated by an end table, a desk, and an adjustable dressmaker's dummy.

"You can hang your coat and winter things on those hooks," Clair said, pointing to a row of hooks on the wall. "I'll need you to take your shoes off and any sweaters or vests, that sort of thing. I need to get an accurate set of measurements from you. Once I have them, I will adjust the dummy to your size, and you can discuss what you want with Rose. We like to design our clothes as close to finish fit as possible. It saves a lot of fitting time that way. I need to get my measuring tape and our design forms. I'll be right back, Miss Halliday."

"Oh, please, call me Ashley."

"All right, Ashley. I'll be right back. Can I bring you anything? Coffee, tea, bottled water?"

"Coffee would be wonderful. One cream and two sugars, please."

"We bring it in on a tray with all the trimmings. That way you can add in whatever you like." She left the room and closed the door.

Ashley set her purse down on one of the chairs and took off her coat, gloves, and scarf. It took a moment to get out of her boots. When Clair returned, she was waiting in the other chair.

Clair came into the room pushing a small tea cart that was painted white, an antique by the looks of it, with metal filigree trimming along the legs and small wooden wheels. On the tray sat two coffee carafes, along with sugar and real cream. Cups made of fine china sat in their own saucers and matched the pattern of the sugar bowl and cream pitcher. Small, silver spoons sat in a crystal holder.

"Here you are, Ashley. Help yourself to the coffee while I get the paperwork started."

Ashley examined the cart. "Where did you get this tea cart?

"Rose bought it at an estate sale last summer. Are you ready?"

A few moments later, Ashley stood on the platform while Clair took her measurements.

Clair was nearly finished when there was a light rap on the door.

"Come in," Clair called out. The door opened, and Rose entered the room.

"Ashley, how lovely to see you." Rose came up and stood beside Clair. "Clair said you wanted a special gown for the Governor's Ball."

"Yes, I do."

"Well then, let me grab my sketchbook, and we can talk about the design while Clair prepares the mannequin." She left the room and returned quickly with an artist's sketchpad and a jar of sharpened drawing pencils. She and Ashley sat down on the chairs, and Ashley told her what she liked while Rose took notes.

An hour later, Rose had an exquisite gown sketched out on her pad, and Ashley smiled approvingly. "I know the ball is in four weeks. I can have the basic dress cut and lightly stitched together by the twenty-first. If you could come in that day and try it on for basic fit and feel, we can put it together and finish it by January fourth. That gives us a few days to make any changes, if necessary, before the ball on the ninth. Is that acceptable?" She looked up and smiled.

"Yes, that would be perfect. Thank you, Rose."

"My pleasure. I'm very pleased you came in to see us." She smiled again.

Ashley smiled back. She reached into her purse and pulled out her iPhone. "I can be here at…" She checked her schedule. "Does eleven work for you?"

Clair left the room and returned with a large day planner. "Yes. We have a wedding fitting in the morning, but we will be finished by then. Eleven will be fine. I'll mark you down."

"Thank you." Ashley stood and reached for her coat. She thought for a moment and then turned to Rose. "Tell Stephen that I got a call from the new aide at the governor's office. The governor sent out special invitations to the ball to a few people on the short list. Stephen will want to know. I'll see you on the twenty-first. Goodbye." She held out her hand, and Rose took it. The two women smiled at each other. Ashley turned and left.

Ashley pulled up her collar against the wind. Only a few snowflakes were falling, but the sky promised more. She hurried around the corner, heading toward her car when she nearly ran into a man coming the other way. "Richard. I'm sorry I didn't see you."

"Ah, the story of my life." He clutched his chest and shook his head and gave her a grin. "What are you doing on this freezing and miserable day?"

Ashley laughed. "Running around town and working. I have another client to see in half an hour. What are you doing out here?"

"Pretty much the same thing. I'm meeting with Stephen in a few minutes to strategize about the bill. If you were free, I'd invite you to participate." He shivered a little. "Are you almost done with your Christmas shopping?"

"I don't have much shopping to do; the family isn't getting together this year." Ashley wiggled her fingers to keep them warm.

"So what are you doing then?" Richard asked, stamping his feet.

"Snuggling up with a good book or binge-watching a television series, I'm not really sure which one." She said with a laugh.

"I'm home alone this year, too. My sister and her family are going on a cruise this year, and I really don't want to join them. Hey, why don't you come over to my house for Christmas Eve dinner? My housekeeper is making a great meal for me before she heads over to her daughter's house; I can tell her to make enough for two people. We can both have some company for part of the holiday. What do you say?" He pulled his scarf higher around his neck.

Ashley thought for a moment. Did she really want to have dinner with Richard? Well, the meal would probably be good, and she really didn't want to spend the entire holiday alone. "Yes, I think I'd like that."

Richard grinned. "Great. I'll see you at my house at six. Now we need to get out of the cold before we freeze to death. Merry Christmas, Ashley."

"Thank you. Merry Christmas, Richard. See you on the twenty-fourth."

Chapter 7
Christmas Eve

"Mrs. Holcomb," Richard bellowed from the kitchen. "What am I supposed to do with the soup?"

A small, plump woman in her late sixties came in from the direction of the dining room. "Mr. Fowler, for the third time, the soup is in the green crockpot and is ready to serve. The salads are chilling in the refrigerator on the left. They are on your grandmother's china, and I wrapped them in cellophane to keep them fresh. The rolls are in the warming oven, and the cauliflower is on the stove, cooking on low. The cheese sauce is in the small blue crockpot. Make sure you don't confuse it with the one containing the soup. When you are ready to serve the cauliflower, put the cauliflower in the china serving bowl I have sitting on the counter next to the stove and pour the sauce over it. The prime rib roast is in the first oven, and the scalloped potatoes are in the second. I have timed them to be done at the same time. When you hear the timers go off, take them out of the oven. The potatoes can stay in the cooking dish, but the roast needs to go on the serving platter. Now the dessert…"

"Mrs. Holcomb, how on earth am I supposed to remember all this? I can barely nuke a TV dinner." Richard ran his fingers through his hair.

"I wrote everything down for you. The paper is over there on the counter next to the liquor cabinet. I figure you'd notice it there."

Richard stared at her for a moment and then started laughing. "Madam, you know me too well." He kept laughing as he walked to the aforementioned cabinet and pulled out a bottle of Glenfiddich.

Mrs. Holcomb shook her head. "Honestly, the way you're carrying on, you'd think the queen was coming for supper."

Richard pulled a glass out of the cabinet and set it on the counter. "You're not far from wrong." He poured himself a generous glass. "Ashley Halliday is not a queen, but she is definitely a princess. I work with her on political issues, and I'd like to keep her as a solid ally at the very least. So I don't want to give her food poisoning or charcoal for her Christmas Eve dinner. I know you've done your part. You're an excellent cook. I, on the other hand, have a tendency to run off on a tangent, and as a result the roast could end up tasting like shoe leather." He took a large swallow of his whiskey.

"Well, keep drinking like that, and you'll be lucky to find the kitchen, let alone the instruction sheet. Now, I've set the dining table, the wine is breathing, and the gas fire is on in the living room, so you don't have to add any wood and get sticky sap all over my clean floors. If there is nothing else you need, I'll be off to my daughter's."

"No, I'll manage Mrs. Holcomb." He reached into his jacket pocket and pulled out an envelope. "Have a Merry Christmas, Mrs. Holcomb, and I'll see you again on Monday."

"Thank you, Mr. Fowler. Merry Christmas to you, and I hope you have a lovely evening with your lady friend." She turned and left the kitchen.

Richard stood there sipping at his drink until he heard the back door close. He still had a half an hour to prepare before Ashley showed up. Time enough to put on some Christmas music and turn on the Christmas tree lights.

Ashley carefully made her way down the hill from her apartment. Her place was actually twenty minutes as the crow flies from Richard's house, but downtown Boise lay between them. Traffic had thinned considerably since this morning, but a wet snowfall had turned the streets into a skating rink. Thank God her Mercedes had front-wheel drive. As she inched her way through the slick streets, she kept wondering if this was really a good idea.

Sure, it would be lonely to spend Christmas Eve alone in her apartment, but she could turn on the television and watch *It's a Wonderful Life* or *A Christmas Story* while drinking a bottle of Merlot. She'd heard her father tell her brothers, "If you're going to drink, never do it alone," many times. Oddly, he had never said it to her. She had always assumed it wasn't the type of advice a father gave his daughter. Maybe he assumed she'd always have a boyfriend or get married early, but he'd never spoken to her about drinking alone. She'd accepted Richard's invitation because her family had abandoned her this holiday season, and she didn't like being alone. Now, as she watched a snowplow go down the other side of the street, that didn't look like a good idea. Sometime this evening, she'd have to navigate these streets again, and they most certainly wouldn't be any less slick. Twice during the journey, she'd reached for her phone on the passenger seat to call and tell Richard she couldn't make it. Undoubtedly, he had a good meal prepared, and canceling at this late date would be the height of rudeness.

She glanced at the external thermometer on her dashboard. The temperature had dropped five degrees since she'd left her house. She'd turned on the defroster as soon as she left, but both side windows were misted over. She wiped her coat sleeve over the driver's side window and glanced out. On Monday, she'd call the dealership and have the car checked over. It shouldn't be fogging up like this.

She turned onto Harrison Boulevard, heading toward Richard's house. Ahead, she could see the antique pole lights that marked the entrance to his driveway. Last chance to call and cancel. No, she'd made it all the way here, might as well have a good meal. After all, she could always go home early with the excuse of bad roads. That way she'd at least have company for a portion of the evening.

Ashley pulled into the driveway and caught a quick movement of the drapes in the front room. He'd been waiting for her, which actually made her feel better. Maybe he was looking forward to having company as well.

The driveway was completely snow- and ice-free. She remembered Stephen telling her that Richard had the driveway redone last year and had installed heat coils to keep it and the walkways clear of ice. The trees and bushes were covered with twinkle lights, and garlands hung around all the posts of the entryway. A huge wreath decorated the front door. The moment she stopped the car, Richard opened the door. He wore dark slacks and an Irish knitted pullover sweater.

"I was beginning to worry. The news said the roads were freezing. I was afraid I'd have to send out a Saint Bernard with a cask of brandy to go search for you. Come in. Come in before you start turning blue."

Ashley laughed. This might just be a good idea after all.

She walked into the entryway and stared. The living room looked like it had been decorated for Christmas by Thomas Kinkade. "Richard, the house is beautiful. You didn't do this yourself, did you?"

"Oh, good Lord, no. I have no sense of decoration at all. My housekeeper, Mrs. Holcomb, does all this with help from the rest of the staff. My grandmother collected Christmas decorations, and a lot of the things on display are her antiques. Grammy loved to decorate for the holidays. It's one of the few family traditions I've kept up. Go ahead and take off your boots. The carpeting is quite plush, and your feet will be plenty warm. Let me take your coat."

"Oh, thank you." Ashley removed her fur-lined gloves and slipped them in her pockets before unbuttoning her coat. She turned and let Richard slide the coat from her shoulders. She removed her woolen scarf and handed that to him as well. While he put her things in the entryway closet, Ashley checked her appearance in the large, gold-framed mirror that hung over a small mahogany cabinet covered with angel statues. She turned to him and smiled. "Well, I must say it looks very festive. I'm glad you invited me."

"Excellent, come this way, and I'll give you a short tour of the different features." She followed him into the main room, and he pointed out some antique Santa and Mrs. Santa dolls, a hand-carved nativity scene, a small, fine-china sled with eight tiny reindeer, and an angel dressed in satin and lace, complete with silk wings. Ashley was particularly impressed with the tree and its decorations, many of which were made of crystal or fine china. The garlands were made of beautiful lace and velvet. Except for the twinkle lights, the room looked like something from another time.

Richard led the way into the dining room. The Christmas decorations in this room matched the ones in the living room. A beautiful hand-painted wooden carousel stood on the hutch. Richard turned the wind-up key, and it began to turn while playing "Good King Wenceslas."

"Richard, this is amazing. Would you mind if I come back with my camera and snap some pictures before you take it down? I could use some of these ideas for next year's Christmas decorations for clients." She touched a porcelain reindeer.

Richard laughed. "Sure, if you like. Everything stays up until after New Year's Eve, so anytime next week would work. Can I offer you a drink to start the evening? Would you like a cocktail or a glass of wine?"

"A cocktail, I'd love a margarita." She gave him a warm smile.

"Right, one margarita coming up. Go ahead and look around while I mix your drink. I'll come and find you when I'm done." He turned and went through a door that she assumed led to the kitchen.

Ashley went back to the living room and sat on the couch. A merry fire burned in the hearth, and her favorite Christmas song, "Carol of the Bells," started playing from speakers that were hidden somewhere behind the decorations. She leaned back and closed her eyes.

Richard came in a few minutes later holding two drinks. He bowed in front of her and handed her the glass. "I hope you like it."

She smiled at him. "Did you make it like your bartender does?"

"More or less," he grinned. "I tend to make them a bit stronger at home. If you don't like it, I can make you another one."

Ashley took a sip. It was stronger but not unpleasant. "It's fine, thank you. Have you made any progress on the land bill?"

Richard briefly told her about starting the data mining and opposition research, careful to make no mention of Jason's involvement or the name of the data company.

By the time he was finished with his explanation, the timers in the kitchen had gone off. They made their way to the dining room. Mrs. Holcomb had placed one table setting at the head of the table and the second one on the side facing the living room. Ashley set her drink down at that spot.

"Do you need any help?" She remained standing in case he said yes. "No. Sit down and enjoy your drink. I'll be back in a few minutes." He disappeared through the kitchen door.

Ashley sat down and looked approvingly at the beautiful table setting. In addition to the elegant china, the glasses were all Waterford crystal. She picked up her wine glass and examined it closely. For the first time she wondered how wealthy Richard actually was.

A beautiful centerpiece of small pine boughs, holly, carnations, and white roses had been placed on the table. She smiled. If her mother were here, she'd be quite impressed.

She looked over at the sideboard and was surprised to see a bottle of Silver Oak cabernet. How did Richard know it was her favorite dinner wine? Had he asked Stephen? Ashley shifted on her chair.

Richard came through the door carrying a basket of rolls and a small bowl of butterballs. Ashley could hear a blender running in the kitchen.

"The prime rib will be ready in just under ten minutes. I thought I'd start bringing out some of the food." He set both items on the table and went back in the kitchen.

Ashley looked at the basket. There were many different kinds of rolls. *There's enough bread here to feed six people.*

Richard returned with another margarita and a plate of salad. He disappeared again, only to come back with his own salad and a special porcelain dish holding several types of salad dressing. Two buzzers went off in the kitchen. "That will be the meat and potatoes." He went out again.

Ashley took a sip of her drink. Whoa. She licked her lips. This margarita was stronger than the first one but still tasty.

It took a little bit longer for Richard to return this time, and he made several more trips in rapid succession. Ashley looked at the dinner spread and smiled. "Richard, this looks absolutely delicious."

Richard grinned. "Thanks. Don't stand on ceremony; go ahead and start while I pour the wine. I think you'll like this; it's my favorite wine with meals."

Ashley spooned some dressing on her salad. "Really? Well, I'll definitely have to try it then." She smiled at her plate. This was turning out to be a very good evening.

Chapter 8

Too Much Holiday Cheer

The different courses went by quickly. Ashley could only eat a little of each dish served. Clearly Richard's housekeeper had planned on having a lot of leftovers. The conversation remained light and pleasant, and Richard made sure her wine glass never stayed empty.

When they finished their meal, they tidied up together. They wrapped the bowls and platters with cellophane and placed the dishes in the refrigerator. Ashley bagged the remaining rolls and poured the soup into a plastic container. Richard filled the sink with warm water while Ashley brought the dishes in from the dining room. She set her plate in the water and glanced out the window. Snow fell rapidly to the ground.

"Oh great! How long has it been snowing that hard?"

Richard came over and stood behind her, looking over her shoulder. "Since we started dinner I believe. I noticed it when I took the meat out of the oven."

"I'm going to have a terrible drive home. I'd better get going now." Ashley turned to leave the kitchen.

"Ashley, wait. The snow is going to be deep, and you said there was a lot of ice on the road when you drove here. Why don't you spend the night? The house has two guest rooms; you can have your pick." He looked concerned.

Ashley bit her lip. She didn't want to stay alone in the house with him, but on the other hand, the roads were going to be treacherous, and she'd had a lot to drink. In the end, practicality won out. "All right, I'll stay. I can wait until the plows have cleared some of the streets before I go back."

Richard smiled. "Good, I'll make you breakfast. It's the only meal I know how to cook." He grinned, and Ashley rolled her eyes.

"Because you're not going anywhere, how about another glass of wine?"

They took their full glasses into the living room and continued their conversation on the couch. Ashley nestled in the corner of the sofa, tucking her feet underneath her. Richard stretched out on the opposite end with his feet resting on an ottoman.

The room looked very cozy and cheerful. Richard had turned off the overhead lights, and the twinkle lights on the tree, the other decorations in the room, and the flickering fireplace were the only lights.

"Richard, when do you think you'll be able to introduce the land bill? Will it be early enough in the session to get it through both houses? And did you figure out which way you want to take the land back?" Ashley took another sip of wine.

"Stephen and I are still gathering information. Depending on what we find, we will either propose to take back the land in increments or force the attorney general to act by lawsuit. Of course, no matter what we do, the biggest obstacle will be Bartlett."

"Which way would you like to go?"

"Well, obviously I'd like to take the land back all at once; doing it piecemeal will be much more expensive. It allows anyone who opposes the idea to file multiple lawsuits on each tract of land. Of course, they can do that anyway, but we stand a better chance of condensing the suits if we go for the whole thing at once."

Ashley shifted on the couch. "Who is doing your data mining?"

"I've hired a company that specializes in data research. There are many reports and news articles that need to be analyzed. Stephen is organizing the legal end. We need to know about all the cases involving federal land. As soon as all the research is in, we will call another meeting to discuss what we've discovered and the best way to proceed."

"Do you have a map in the house that shows where the federal land is in the state? I'd like to consult it while we talk."

"Yes. I had a very accurate one made by a local mapping company. It shows the location of the land and the county it's in. It also shows the percentage of federal land versus private land in each county. That information is of particular concern to the various county commissioners. I plan to have the support of as many of them as possible when the bill is presented. Anyway, the map also shows the location of all the roads and other access points. Would you like me to get it now?" He removed his feet from the ottoman and leaned forward.

"Oh, I'd love to see it, but first I need to find your powder room." She blushed a little. "I've had quite a lot of wine."

He laughed. "Around the corner and first door on your left. I'll get the computer while you're busy."

Ashley got up and left the room. Richard walked down the hallway to his office and took the laptop from the desk. He opened a drawer and pulled out an envelope containing a letter and a thumb drive.

When Ashley returned, she found Richard had moved the coffee table closer to the sofa and set up his computer in the middle of it. He stared at the screen while typing at the keyboard. She'd known Richard for about two years as a friend, an ally, and a very shrewd and calculating political player, but she had never really looked at him as a man. Watching him sitting on his sofa completely relaxed, he didn't seem so guarded or distant. He had a boyish grin on his face. His thick, brown hair looked ruffled instead of immaculately groomed.

Richard looked up and smiled at her. She felt embarrassed to be caught staring at him.

"I got the program up and running. Come sit down, and I'll show it to you."

She walked over and sat beside him. There was a refilled glass of wine in front of her on the table.

"See, this is how the program works." Richard demonstrated all the special keys and commands that showed all the federal land in the state. The map had amazing detail. It not only showed the size of the various land pockets but also the topography. The program was obviously expensive to create. Ashley wondered how much Richard had paid for it. She laughed as he described another new feature. He looked and sounded like a kid with a new toy.

He turned and looked at her. "Hey, I had this designed so that even members of the senate could understand what we are trying to do."

Ashley reached over and lightly slapped him on the shoulder.

Richard grabbed her wrist and held it. "Why Senator Halliday, is that any way to react to a conference committee presentation?"

She laughed and tried to pull back her arm, but he wouldn't let go. "Richard…"

Her protest was cut off when he put his mouth on hers and kissed her. His lips were warm, and he tasted sweet and sour, a combination of the wine and whiskey. Her initial shock at the kiss changed quickly to something else. He broke off the kiss and pulled back, looking at her face.

She could read the question in his eyes: Had he made a mistake? She closed her eyes and leaned forward. His lips met hers again. A small voice in her mind asked what she was doing. This was Richard Fowler, a friend and political ally, not a boyfriend or lover. Her body seemed to overrule that comment. She hadn't been held or kissed by a man in a long time, and it felt so good.

His arms came around her, and he deepened the kiss as "Silent Night" played. She reached up and pulled him closer. He moved his mouth along her jawline, kissing his way toward her neck. She shivered as he suckled her earlobe, his tongue playing with her diamond stud earring. He gently guided her body until she lay stretched out along the couch, Richard kneeling beside her and running kisses down her neck toward her breasts. He stopped and looked into her eyes. She knew he was looking for permission to continue. She made the decision without thinking and reached up, pulling him down for another kiss.

Ashley woke in a strange bed. The room was still dark, but her internal clock told her it was around seven in the morning and time to get up. The sheets felt soft against her skin. Her eyes flew open. She wasn't wearing a stitch of clothing. Then she noticed the soft snoring coming from the other side of the bed, and the memory of the night before came back to her with a jolt; Richard and his

Christmas dinner, the wine, the music, and that kiss. She slowly moved, trying to sit up without waking him. There was a pain in her temples and behind her eyes. How much wine had she drunk last night? It would have been easy to blame everything on the wine, but Ashley had to be more honest than that. She had wanted last night. She could easily have said no. The house, the decorations, the food, everything had contributed to the evening. It was the kiss; she could still feel it on her lips. That kiss changed everything. The rest of the sensations came flooding back in memory. Richard was a very good lover. That made her blush. How was she supposed to act around him now?

The first thing she needed to do was get out of his house. She couldn't face him, not yet anyway. She carefully slid off the bed. It wasn't an easy task, finding her clothes in the dark, but she managed and tiptoed to the bedroom door. Thank goodness the hinges were well oiled; the door opened silently. She made her way down the stairs to the powder room she'd used the night before. The lights from the Christmas displays were off. She raised an eyebrow. Richard hadn't turned them off last night; they must be on a timer.

Ashley dressed quickly and stepped out of the front door. Her car stood under the entryway, protected from last night's snowfall. In a few minutes, she was heading for home.

Richard felt the bed stir when Ashley woke. He remained quiet, wanting her to think he was still asleep. He heard her shuffle about the room looking for her clothes. He smiled. He could almost feel the warmth from her flushed cheeks as she tiptoed out of the bedroom. She'd be embarrassed for now, but he'd make sure their next meeting was very pleasant. Last night had been a complete surprise. They'd known each other for nearly two years. Of course, she was Stephen's girlfriend for most of that time, but still he always thought of her as special.

He rolled over and tapped the alarm code into the keypad by his bed. If she wanted to sneak out of his house, then having the burglar alarm go off would really cause problems. He wanted to see her again, but he would need to give her time.

Chapter 9

New Year's Eve

Ashley stood in front of her bathroom mirror, putting on her diamond and sapphire earrings, along with her matching necklace. Tonight's New Year's Eve party marked the first time in a week that she'd be out in public.

"Oh, come on."

Her left earring was being difficult, or maybe it was the shaking of her fingers.

Since Christmas she'd stayed in her apartment, only answering calls from clients and working on her design projects. The one exception was the day she answered the door to find a deliveryman from a florist. He brought a spectacular floral arrangement of white and pink lilies mixed with red and pink roses and assorted greenery. All the flowers rested in an etched crystal vase. The card simply said, "Happy New Year, Richard."

Ashley closed her eyes; thank goodness her parents were still in Hawaii. She didn't want to have to explain to her mother why Richard had sent her flowers.

She opened her eyes and took a deep breath; tomorrow was the first day of the new year, a time for new beginnings and fresh starts. Tonight she'd celebrate that fact at a party. Ashley checked her face in the mirror, no wrinkles or crow's feet yet. She closed her eyes and sighed. This new year would be better than the last one; after all, she was a state senator now. The first day of the session was in two weeks, and she would take her place in the legislature. The possibility that Bartlett would name her lieutenant governor hovered over her head like an exotic butterfly, tempting and marvelous but just beyond her reach. She glanced at the flowers and shivered. What else would the new year bring? Well, she wouldn't find out standing here looking into a mirror. "Mirror, mirror on the wall" only worked in fairy tales. It was time to drive to the party and see where life would lead.

"Bartlett is really playing his choice for lieutenant governor close to the vest. I have talked to several of his closest advisers and staff, but no one has a clue about who is rising to the top of the list." Morgan Tate took another sip of his drink. "Have you heard anything, Richard?"

Richard set his glass down on a side table near the fireplace. "I've seen a copy of the short list, but given that it's Bartlett, I wouldn't be surprised if he picked someone who is not even on the list. The only thing I'm sure of is whoever he picks will be his puppet. He won't risk losing his legacy by having the leader of the senate undermining his policies."

Morgan nodded. "You're probably right. You know your dad never trusted him. Years ago, when Bartlett was a county commissioner, he offered to help us get the proper zoning for that shopping mall we built out on Overland Street. Your father politely turned down his offer. He knew there would be a price to pay for Bartlett's help, and it was probably more of a debt than we would want hanging over our heads."

Morgan took another sip of his drink. "I really miss your dad. He was a great man and a good friend. I know he'd be proud of you being in the legislature."

Richard hastily picked up his glass and took a drink. Talking about his dad always made him uncomfortable. This would be a good time for some other party guest to interrupt, but no such luck.

Morgan nodded his head and then looked at Richard. "I know he'd be disappointed that you never had kids. He always wanted grandkids."

Richard nearly choked. "When did he say that? Oh, never mind. Sheesh, you make it sound like I'm old and over the hill. I'm only thirty-four."

Morgan laughed. "You're not old, but face it, son, you've been married twice, and, well, I'm just saying he always wanted grandchildren."

At that moment, the doorbell rang. Morgan's wife, Ann, opened the door to reveal Ashley standing on the step. Richard quickly turned his back to the door. "Morgan, I think I'll go and refresh my drink. Will you excuse me?"

Morgan smiled. "Certainly, we'll talk later." The old man turned and wandered over to another group of people.

Richard made his way to the bar. He didn't intend to refresh his drink; the location of the bar made it easy to survey the party and watch the other people move through the rooms. He wasn't quite ready for Ashley to see him. His father's words echoed in his mind. "Pursuing a high-spirited woman is like hunting a deer. You need to be very careful and slowly get close, so you don't spook her; you can't catch her if you can't get close." Ashley was definitely spooked. The thank-you note she sent him for the flowers proved that. The key to the situation was simple; make their first meeting after Christmas a pleasant and fun experience to overcome the awkwardness. When Morgan invited him to the party, he'd asked that Ashley be invited as well. It was an easy request because Morgan knew both of her parents well. Now that he had set up their first meeting, what was the best way to proceed?

Ashley gave the hostess her coat. She set her snow boots on the door rack next to the ones left by the other guests and carefully slipped into the pumps that went with her party dress. Morgan Tate was an old friend of her father's, but this was the first time she'd attended his annual New Year's Eve party. Quite a few of Boise's prominent citizens were here. The mayor stood in a corner conversing with a county commissioner and the CEO of a local electronics company. The anchorman from the six o'clock news stood with the director of the art museum and a real estate developer. Many more people filled the living, dining, and television rooms of the house. Ashley gave the rest of the crowd a quick scan but didn't see any members of the legislature. Good, this would be a nice social evening with no political players in the house.

Ann returned. "I'm so glad you could make it this year, Ashley. I understand your parents are still in Hawaii."

"Yes, my mother called last night. They are having a wonderful time. I think she'd like to talk my dad into retiring there."

Ann laughed. "That will never happen. He may buy a condo there and visit, but you'll never get him to leave Boise. For that matter, I don't think she'll be able to get him to retire. He loves arguing in court. I think he'll keep doing it as long as he can still walk into a courtroom."

Ashley laughed. "You're probably right, but my mother can be quite persuasive. Thank you so much, Ann, for inviting me here this evening."

"Oh, nonsense. You know you and your family are always welcome in our home. Now I'm sure you already know all of our guests. If there's anyone you don't know, then come find me, and I'll introduce you."

"Thank you, Ann."

Ann gave her a warm smile and went over to a group of ladies standing by the sliding glass doors to the patio.

Ashley took a deep breath and walked over to the nearest group of people.

Richard watched Ashley for a while, admiring her beauty. She looked so elegant in her dress. He smiled. He'd always appreciated her beauty, and he liked the way she carried herself. A flash of their Christmas evening together ran through his mind. He closed his eyes. He couldn't let memories of that evening float freely in his head. Already a lot of the blood necessary to hold an intelligent conversation was rushing to another part of his anatomy.

Slow. That was the operative word for the evening, slow and careful.

Richard opened his eyes and saw the sparkle in Ashley's. She stood deep in conversation with the mayor. He was sure she was telling him about the upcoming legislative session and what she hoped to accomplish. She really was remarkable. He nodded his head; time to start working the room until he came face to face with the charming Miss Halliday.

He moved carefully around from group to group, speaking to different people and always making sure he was not in her direct line of sight. Let her relax first and feel comfortable and then go up to her and say hello.

Half an hour later, they still hadn't met. Richard stayed in the vicinity of the bar, knowing she would get thirsty and work her way there eventually. It would be easier to break the ice while he was literally breaking the ice, for her drink.

His opportunity came when Morgan asked him to make a mai tai the way they did at his bar. He returned with the drink just as Ashley walked up to join the group Morgan was talking to.

Ashley moved closer to Morgan's group just in time to hear the mayor explain the proposed downtown parking plan. She turned to ask Morgan a question and froze. Richard stood there with a smile on his face. He handed Morgan a drink.

"Ashley, it's great to see you. Happy New Year," he said. "What would you like to drink?"

She didn't know what to say. Morgan frowned at her and looked like he was about to ask her what was wrong.

Richard stepped in to break the awkward moment. "How about a glass of wine? There's a really nice Merlot behind the bar. I'll get you a glass." He turned and headed back to the bar.

His question and departure gave her enough time to compose herself. "Mr. Mayor, won't your parking proposal add an extra cost for the downtown merchants? I mean, with the limited parking there is, an increase in the cost to park in the city-run lots will drive even more shoppers to the malls unless the merchants validate the parking."

Morgan laughed, and the mayor turned red.

Morgan put his arm around her shoulder. "I've been telling him the same thing for the last hour."

Ashley grinned. "Mr. Mayor, you have to look for a different source of revenue or cut the city budget. If you keep squeezing the businesses in the downtown area, all that will happen is they will move to the malls outside the city limits."

Ann joined the group. "Enough of the political talk; it's New Year's. Now let's talk about pleasant things. Who needs another drink?"

Richard walked up and handed Ashley a large glass of wine. "I'll mix any drinks needed."

Ann stroked his arm. "Richard, you are a dear. Can you make me a piña colada?"

"Of course I can. What kind of bartender do you think I am? Any other orders?"

Several guests came over and placed their orders. Richard repeated each order out loud and went to the bar. Ashley waited a few minutes and followed him.

He stood at the bar with a shaker in his hand making a martini.

She hesitated, not quite knowing what to say.

Richard grinned at her and started dancing with the shaker in a way that made her laugh.

"Do you like the Merlot?" He opened the shaker and filled two martini glasses.

"It's very good, but I think I'd like something stronger." She set the wine glass on the bar.

"Your wish is my command. What would you like me to make for you?"

"I'm not sure. I'd like something tropical … hmm … how about Sex on the Beach?" The moment she said the words, she wanted to rip her tongue out.

Richard didn't laugh at her or give her a knowing look. He simply turned around and grabbed a bottle of peach schnapps. "Do you want Ketel One or Grey Goose as your vodka of choice?"

The party settled down to a normal rhythm, with lots of small talk but no more politics. At a quarter of an hour 'til midnight, Ann asked Richard and Ashley to help pass out champagne to all the guests. Ann opened the sheers in the large bay windows, giving a clear view of the city below. With one minute left in the old year, the guests began the countdown. Richard stood beside Ashley, both of them watching the lights of the city. "Three … Two … One … Happy New Year." The room filled with voices as people wished each other good will for the coming year. Outside, the fireworks blossomed over the city. Neither Richard nor Ashley paid any attention. They were locked in each other's arms, each giving and receiving a New Year's kiss.

Chapter 10
Dreams

John paced his plot. Not an easy task considering it was only seven feet long and four feet wide. What could she possibly be doing? It had to be around three in the morning. He stopped when he reached the headstone and leaned on it. Abaddon wanted him to walk in her dreams again, but she needed to be asleep before that could happen. He struck his hand against the stone. Women in this time were so different from what he was used to. Everything in this time was strange. Abaddon had explained the changes and taught him what to expect, but the reality of seeing all the new things people had invented and the different ways men and women reacted to each other left him uncomfortable.

John glanced up at the stars. He could barely see them because of the electric lights from the city. How many times in his life had he looked up at those same stars and watched their progress through the seasons? Now, he couldn't find anything familiar. Abaddon had said if he completed his assignment, he would be able to live again. He hoped that meant in his own time. John couldn't imagine living in this time. In truth, the thought frightened him.

A dark mist surrounded him, and he heard Abaddon speak, "She's home; prepare to go to her."

It took almost an hour before he was able to step out of the mirror. He walked straight to the bed and kneeled beside Ashley. Having learned his lesson the last time, he got right down to business. At least the long wait wasn't completely wasted. He'd spent a lot of time deciding where to take her in the dream world. Abaddon wanted her to be very comfortable with John at the

Governor's Ball, so the most logical thing was to get her used to dancing with him. That made him think of the party his parents had put together in honor of his graduation from Harvard. It was a beautiful summer night, and all the guests had gathered in the backyard of the family home. Yes, that was the perfect memory to use.

It was also the night he danced with Rose Van Buren for the first time. It would be nice to see her again in her pretty dress. That was a pleasant time; he was free to be with any woman he pleased. Felicia, now there was a friendly woman. He probably should have married her. That's what his family had wanted, but while she was fun and very willing, she wasn't really appealing to him other than her obvious charms. Not like Rose, who stood out in a crowd like a candle in a dark room.

He took a deep breath. What would be the best time to enter the party? Probably not when he actually had been there dancing with some of the ladies. No, the best time would be when he'd stolen upstairs with Felicia; that way there would not be two of him on the dance floor, and Ashley would not be frightened. John closed his eyes and concentrated.

Ashley's dream wasn't a pleasant one. Her oldest brother was telling her she had to marry Senator Albright, for the good of the family. She kept telling him that Albright was old enough to be their grandfather, and he couldn't possibly help the family, but it didn't make a difference. She was about to run away from him when John came to the door.

"I'm here to take you to the ball."

Ashley didn't remember changing her clothes or traveling, but she found herself standing in a beautiful backyard decorated for a party. The yard was filled with people dressed in their finest. Wait a minute; the clothes...it looked like a scene from some movie about the 1800s. Women were dressed in long flowing gowns with their hair all done up. She looked at her own clothes and discovered she was also wearing a costume.

I look like Scarlett O'Hara. She glanced around again. Paper lanterns hung in the trees. Chairs lined the edges of the vast lawn, several occupied by party guests. A small group of musicians sat on chairs tucked into a specially designed recess in the shrubbery, playing music while some guests danced on the large grassy open space in the center. Against the wall of the house, servants tended buffet tables laden with delicacies. Two waiters stood at a table filling their trays with glasses of Champagne to carry out among the crowd.

Butterflies were fluttering in her stomach. She'd never had such a detailed dream before. Beside her, John grabbed two glasses of Champagne and handed her one.

"Isn't it a beautiful night?" He took a sip.

Ashley looked around. It really was a beautiful evening. She couldn't remember seeing so many stars in the sky. The details in this dream were amazing.

"Would you like to dance?"

She turned to see John smiling at her. He really had a great smile. "Sure."

He took her glass and placed it with his on the tray of a passing waiter, and then he took her hand and led her to the center of the lawn.

John stole a quick glance at her breasts. The dress fit her tightly, making both orbs push up enticingly from the bodice of her gown. He stopped on the dance floor and held her right hand up while sliding his other arm around her waist and pulling her close. She rested her free hand on his shoulder, and he waltzed her around the lawn.

He smiled. Ashley was a good dancer. He looked up and saw Rose dancing with the brewer's son. All these years, and he was still jealous of any other man touching her. His displeasure must have shown on his face. Ashley wrinkled her brow. "Is something wrong?"

"Oh no, everything is fine." He gave her a warm smile, and she seemed to relax. They moved around the dance floor, John making sure that Ashley always had her back to Rose. This way he could keep an eye on his late wife. Was that what she was? Well, it didn't really matter, as long as he could keep an eye on Rose without alerting or alarming Ashley or allowing Ashley to see her.

"So tell me, Ashley, how did you get into politics?"

Ashley laughed. "It's a long story."

"That's all right; we have all night."

Ashley was pleasantly surprised that John was such an excellent dancer. He'd led her expertly around the dance floor and didn't step on her toes once. He was also a good listener, making only a few comments while she told him about her decision to go into politics.

She wasn't sure how long they'd been dancing when John announced that it was time to take her home. He led her quickly off the dance floor, and she had the feeling he was in a hurry. She turned to take one last look at the party and the lovely backyard and froze. There in the middle of the lawn was another John, and he was dancing with Rose Winship. She turned to speak to the John beside her and managed to say, "What?" before waking up in her bedroom.

"Turn to your left, please, Ashley." Clair, the assistant, placed another pin in the hem of the dress. Ashley looked at her reflection. The gown Rose had designed was truly stunning, a smooth full-length dress with elegant embroidery over the bodice and down the sides, disappearing at the hip.

"Ashley, hold up your right arm, so I can adjust the sleeves and the shoulder drape." Rose pulled a pin from her wrist cushion. "Do you like the color?"

"It's beautiful. You truly are a gifted designer." Ashley ran her free hand over her flat stomach. "What is this color called?"

Rose smiled. "Creamy Mist; it was a very popular color in the late 1800s."

Clair stood up. "It's the perfect color for you. It compliments your hair and complexion."

A waltz sounded through the room. Ashley swayed in front of the mirrors. The movements of the cloth looked graceful, and she imagined how she'd look dancing in it at the Governor's Ball.

She closed her eyes and saw the capitol building, decorated and full of people. Couples danced in the center of the rotunda; others sat at the tables scattered around the perimeter. A man called her name, and she turned to see John from the governor's office holding out his hand and asking her to dance.

Her eyes flew open. This had to do with that crazy dream she had last night. She turned to see whether Rose or Clair had noticed anything. Rose stood at the table making notes in a book, and Clair had her back to the mirror, sticking more pins in her wrist pinholder. This dreaming and thinking of John had to stop. She took a deep breath and examined the dress again.

The gown was exactly want she wanted for the occasion, rich and elegant, complimenting her figure and looking like it was designed for royalty.

"When will it be ready?" Ashley turned toward Rose.

"With the adjustments from this fitting, we can have it finished by…" She glanced at her assistant. "Clair, do you think we can do it by Tuesday?"

"Oh, easily. Ashley, can I get you to stand facing the mirror, so I can get the last of this hem pinned?"

"Stephen, Charlie Montgomery is here to see you," Amanda, his receptionist, announced over the intercom.

"Send him in." Stephen hastily closed the files on his desk and stuffed them in a drawer. He smiled. It had been more than a year since Senator Albert Bellmore had suggested that Stephen become Charlie's mentor. Charlie's father had abandoned his family, and the senator worked with an organization that tried to help at-risk kids. Since that time, Stephen and Charlie had gotten together every other Saturday to play racquetball at the gym. Charlie loved politics and helped with Stephen's campaigns. The boy's attitude and grades had improved remarkably since then

Charlie bounded into the room. "Hey Stephen," he said, and plopped into a chair.

"Hey, sport. How was school today?"

Amanda walked into the office and handed Charlie a soda. "Here you go."

"Thanks, Miss Halpern," Charlie shouted to her as she headed back down the hall.

Stephen grinned. Charlie was a great kid, and all the women in his office fussed over him like a flock of mother hens.

"Ah, school was school; I got a 'B' on the math test, so that's okay. Oh, I tried out for the debate team. The teacher really liked my argument about last year's grocery tax bill. I think I made the team, but I won't find out for sure until Thursday." He opened the can and guzzled down half of it.

"A 'B' grade isn't bad, especially since it was only three weeks ago that you didn't even understand the algebra homework." Stephen shifted in his chair. "Mandy called and said you'd be by to pick up the key to the new campaign headquarters. Is she working you hard to get everything ready for next week?" He was very glad that his campaign manager and Charlie got along so well.

"Yeah, she asked me to get a couple of friends to meet us there today. She has some furniture coming, and we need help getting things set up." He took another swig from the can.

"So when do I get to see the finished product?"

Charlie grinned. "Patience. You can see it when we're finished."

Stephen laughed. Charlie had jumped into the world of politics and really liked the water. Stephen reached into his desk, pulled out a small, key ring, and placed it on the desktop. "The key with the blue tab is for the regular lock; the one with the yellow tab is for the deadbolt."

Charlie reached over and grabbed the keys. "Okay, I'll give the keys to Mandy as soon as she gets there. I'm heading over now, so I can finish cleaning the backroom. Oh, yeah, I talked to my mom, and she's giving me a note to get out of my last two classes, so I can be at your official announcement. I'll take my sports coat and tie with me, so I'll fit in. Mandy is picking me up at school and driving me over." He stood up, drained the last of the can, and placed it on the desk. "See you at the regular time for racquetball on Saturday?"

"Yup, I'll pick you up at nine."

Amanda's voice came over the intercom. "Stephen, Tabitha Kendrick is calling for you on line four."

"I'd better get going. I'll see you Saturday."

"Be careful, Charlie."

"I will." Charlie waved and left the room.

Stephen picked up the phone. "Ms. Kendrick, thank you for calling. I take it you found some information."

"Hello, Mr. Winship. I only just started my research, but I thought you'd want to hear this right away."

"Okay."

"John Jacob Leeds died on April 12, 1890. Mr. Winship, he was murdered."

Chapter 11
The Governor's Ball

John leaned against the frame of the mirror with his hands folded over his chest, waiting. He hated waiting. He had no patience when he was alive and hadn't improved in death. Abaddon wanted John to observe the party before he would allow him to participate. That was probably a good idea. There were lots of people standing around talking to one another, while others danced to the strange music. John didn't recognize anyone except the governor and Radnor.

His mirror was located near one of the liquor carts, which was doing a brisk business. Politics hadn't really changed much since his day.

Bartlett stood a few feet away in the other direction. John could hear him greet the newcomers, and he tried to memorize the names and faces.

John also had a good view of the dance floor. The dances from his time were more complicated and required greater skill. He watched the dancers, imitating their movements while he waited. He'd always been a good dancer and picked up new steps quickly. It wouldn't do to crush Ashley's toes when he took her out on the floor.

He sighed. Change the music and the people's attire, and this could have been one of the political gatherings he'd attended in his own time. He'd been to quite a few of them. After all, he was being groomed to be the first governor when Idaho became a state. John took a deep breath and looked down at the floor. All of that ended because of Rose and the scandal in the wake of her death.

He shook his head. Well, there was nothing he could do about it now. Still, the thoughts of what could have been plagued him.

He glanced around the room again. Where was Ashley, and why was she late? He tapped his foot. That was another thing. Abaddon had given him new instructions to dance with Ashley only once and devote most of his attention to the governor's daughter. The governor's daughter? He'd never even seen her before. He had only found out this morning that she was supposed to come to the ball tonight. Radnor had been telling Hampton about her while they were going over some last-minute preparations for the evening's events. There was a problem with her school back east. She'd come home, and they were setting her up to work in her father's office while continuing her education at Boise State. John wanted to ask Abaddon what this was all about, but Abaddon didn't strike him as the type to explain anything.

A new person came up to the governor and shook his hand. It was one of the state's congressmen. John concentrated on the conversation. While the two men were speaking, a third walked up. The man turned out to be one of the state's U.S. senators. That was interesting. Idaho was still a territory in his time and had no representation in Washington. Truth be told, he would have preferred being a senator or congressman to being a governor. He loved the East Coast. The years he spent there going to school were the happiest times of his life. No responsibilities or worries about the family mining business, and especially no meddling or interfering by his domineering mother.

His thoughts were interrupted by the appearance of the governor's wife, Sarah, and a young woman whom he assumed must be their daughter, Rachel. The sight of Sarah made him shiver. She reminded him of his own mother. Not in appearance, Sarah Bartlett barely reached five feet in height. It was in their personalities. Cold, shrewd, and calculating—none of which was high on the list of motherly virtues. That brought his attention to Rachel. She was pretty and looked to be in her early twenties. Rachel stood several inches above her mother, obviously inheriting some of her father's height. She wore a light-green gown. The coloring went well with her soft brown hair. The governor seemed delighted to see her; she was obviously Daddy's little girl.

A movement in front of the mirror caught his attention. Ashley walked past him looking like a queen. He shook his head. Abaddon might want him to pay special attention to Rachel, but he was definitely dancing with Ashley more than once.

Ashley took a deep breath and then walked over to the governor's group. A lot was riding on making a good impression tonight. Bartlett needed to name his new lieutenant governor soon because the legislative session would start next week. The senate could function for a while with the majority leader acting as the pro tem, but Bartlett would need to name someone before the end of January. After that, there would be too many bills and other business, and a permanent president pro tempore, or pro tem for short, would need to be in place.

"Good evening, Governor, Mrs. Bartlett." She nodded to each one in turn.

Bartlett held out his hand. "Ashley, I'm delighted you could come. Allow me to introduce my daughter, Rachel. Rachel this is Senator Ashley Halliday. Rachel has come home from back east and will be working in my office."

"Really? Well Rachel, I'm sure I'll be seeing a lot of you around the capitol."

Sarah looked Ashley up and down. "Ashley, what a stunning dress; where did you get it? It looks like it came from Paris."

"Oh, thank you, Mrs. Bartlett." Ashley didn't want to tell her that Rose Winship had designed the dress. Stephen's grocery tax bill last session made him public enemy number one as far as the Bartletts were concerned. The fact that he would announce his bid for the governor's office and try to defeat Bartlett wasn't going to improve their opinion of him. Best not remind them that Stephen was at one time her fiancé, and they were still good friends.

"Ashley, I heard a rumor that some members of the house are looking into having the state take over the federal lands within our borders. Have you heard anything about this?" Bartlett gave her a warm, fatherly smile.

The bustline of her dress suddenly felt two sizes too small. How in the world had he found out about it? She couldn't very well tell him she knew nothing about it and then end up being the senate sponsor of the bill. She kept her face blank. "I heard that rumor as well and found it a curious idea. I was going to look into it after the session started."

Bartlett looked like he was about to say something else on the subject when he was interrupted by the arrival of one of Idaho's U.S. senators. Ashley took the opportunity to excuse herself and went off to find one of the liquor carts. She could use a good stiff drink.

Richard stood a few feet behind the governor talking to Stephen. They both watched Ashley and her exchange with Bartlett.

Stephen shook his head. "How the hell did he find out?"

Richard gestured to Stephen and they walked to the opposite side of the room. Rose followed them. "The only thing I can think of is he has people watching the state archives, and someone tipped him about our research into fires and management on federal lands. He put two and two together and figured someone wants to take the land back. I may not like the guy, but I have to admire his intelligence network and his ability to put together a picture from the puzzle pieces." Richard took another sip of his whiskey.

"So what should we do about the situation?" Stephen reached down and took Rose's hand.

Richard smiled. It was good to see his friend happy in his marriage. "Nothing. All he knows is someone is doing research. He doesn't know who ordered it. I think I'll throw a red herring into the mix. I can ask the data miners to research a totally different subject and give him something else to worry about. Remember the story about the Chinese government buying land out by the state penitentiary? He was involved in that up to his eyeballs. I can get them poking through all the contracts and sale information. That should distract him for a bit. It might also give you another issue for your campaign." Richard emptied his glass.

Rose turned to her husband. "Stephen, I'm getting thirsty. Can we get something to drink?"

"Sure, love. You'll excuse us, Richard. We'll meet up again after we've worked the room."

"Yeah, I'll head over to Ashley and see if I can have a discrete word with her. We'll definitely talk later."

Ashley could see Richard eyeing her up and down as he made his way over to where she stood. The look he gave her made her cheeks flush and gave her interesting sensations in more private places.

He stopped in front of her and smiled. "You look stunning. If we were in a different place, I'd take you in my arms and kiss you."

She laughed. "That would turn a few heads. Richard, did you hear what Bartlett asked me? How does he know?"

"I don't think he does. I figure he's been tipped off about the information searches the data miners are doing, but there is no way he can know who their client is. I talked to Stephen about a plan to put in a red herring for him to find. Don't worry about anything; we have it covered." He grinned at her. "Would a beautiful senator be willing to dance with a lowly representative?"

"Of course I will." She held out her hand. It tingled at his touch as he led her away to the dance floor.

It felt good to be in his arms. The motion of his body against hers brought back the memories of Christmas Eve. She looked into his eyes and knew he was remembering the same thing. She gave him a meaningful smile, and he grinned back. They had to be careful; Bartlett or one of his staff was probably watching them with interest.

"Are you looking forward to the session starting on Monday?" He twirled her around so her back was to Bartlett.

Clever. This way, Bartlett couldn't read her lips. "I'm excited and nervous at the same time. I went to the orientation and have some idea of what to expect, but, well, you never know, do you?"

Richard twirled her again. "Would you like to meet me for lunch at my bar after the morning session? They usually recess after the governor's state of the state speech."

She smiled. "I'd love to. I'll meet you in the rotunda when the pro tem releases us, and we can walk over together."

"It's a date, Senator Halliday."

The band started a new song, and Richard led her in the foxtrot. At the end, they walked to the tables at the edge of the dance floor.

"Where did you learn to dance like that?" Ashley said, her breathing still heavy.

"Dance lessons since age ten." Richard pulled out a chair for her.

"Really, who taught you?"

"My mother insisted that my sister and I learn how to dance for all social occasions. My father had two left feet, and I was her partner at most of the parties they threw."

"I'm glad she did. I love dancing." She glanced around. "I think we'd better separate for a while. We seem to be gathering some unwanted attention." She motioned over to Radnor, who was rudely staring at the two of them.

"Good idea. I'll see you on Monday." He smiled and stood up. "Have a pleasant evening, Senator Halliday."

John felt the pressure drop in the mirror. Abaddon was releasing him, finally. He materialized in a niche near the entrance to the ballroom. No one was around, and he straightened his tuxedo. At least Abaddon dressed him well for his assignments.

He wandered around the corner looking for Ashley and spotted her walking to the far end of the ballroom with that annoying fellow from the house, Richard Fowler. They disappeared when they stepped into the shadows, and his eyes could not penetrate the darker perimeter of the room. To go after her, he'd have to walk past the governor, and that wouldn't look good. Might as well spend some time with Rachel and catch up to Ashley later.

After she'd left Richard, Ashley carefully worked the room. She'd spoken to several of the senators present, as well as the chairmen of the two committees she'd be serving on. There were so many compliments about her dress, she was sure Rose would see a marked increase in her business as a result.

Ashley kept glancing back to where Bartlett stood holding court and keeping careful tabs on each of the other senators on Bartlett's short list. He didn't seem to pay a great amount of attention to any of them. In fact, Hampton didn't go near him all night, and she could have sworn those two were joined at the hip.

John was there. He kept talking to the governor's daughter in the corner of the room. Perhaps Bartlett had asked him to pay attention to Rachel because he was the only member of the governor's staff close to her age.

The room was warm, and a glass of wine sounded perfect. Ashley made her way to one of the liquor carts. She was just about to order a white wine when John came up beside her.

"Is this a good time for that dance?" he asked and held out his hand.

Ashley smiled. "That would be lovely." She couldn't help but remember her dream and was curious to see if he danced as well in person.

Rose sat at one of the tables on the edge of the dance floor, sipping a glass of ginger ale. The room was warm, and her stomach felt a little queasy. It was probably the excitement and her pregnancy, but she didn't want to say anything to Stephen. This event was important to him, and he needed to speak to several people in the room. When he announced his candidacy next week, he would be calling a lot of these people for money and support. Rose didn't want him to miss the opportunity simply because she wasn't feeling well. She had told him her feet hurt, and she needed to sit down for a while. That was the truth, but it wasn't the whole truth.

Rose took another sip from her glass and looked around the room. Stephen stood with Richard talking to a group of businessmen. The governor was busy talking to the U.S. senators. Rose wondered what the governor would do when Stephen announced his plan to run against him. She shivered, not wanting to think of all the things Bartlett could do. He'd proven how ruthless he was with the tax bill last year.

She continued to scan the room for people she knew. Her eyes crossed to the dance floor, and her heart leaped into her throat. Her fingers couldn't hold her glass, and the ginger ale spilled on the tablecloth. There, in the middle of the dance floor, was Ashley

Halliday in the arms of the man who had betrayed Rose and caused her death, her ex-husband, John Jacob Leeds.

Stephen didn't believe for an instant that Rose wanted to sit because her feet hurt. He'd been watching her closely all night. Something was wrong; he was sure of it. He'd asked her several times if she wanted to go home. He could always call these people and meet with them privately. If she weren't feeling well, then they would leave. Nothing was more important to him than his wife. She'd steadfastly refused, saying she was fine, only tired because of the pregnancy. He kept glancing in her direction just the same.

Richard had introduced him to Sam and Paul Miller. Paul seemed like a nice guy, and Stephen had offered to help him with his first few weeks in the legislature. After all, it took a while to learn the rules and protocols. It was fascinating to hear how their company operated and how they did their analyses. Richard had just made another joke when Stephen turned to see how Rose was doing. He nearly dropped his drink. She sat at the table, white as a sheet and staring in front of her. He quickly excused himself.

"Rose, sweetheart, what is it? What's wrong?" Stephen asked.

She didn't answer. She was shaking from head to foot and staring in front of her.

"Rose, Rose, please, what's wrong?"

She raised a trembling hand and pointed at the dance floor.

He followed her pointing finger and saw John spin Ashley around the floor. At the same moment, John looked over and saw Rose.

John's face mirrored the look of horror on his own. John controlled it better though, continuing to dance with Ashley as he stared at his late wife.

Stephen helped Rose to her feet and kept whispering in her ear. "It will be all right. I won't let him hurt you. It will be all right."

They hurried out of the room.

John couldn't believe his eyes. Rose. Here. In this time. Alive. And who was the man with her?

Demon or not, Abaddon was going to answer some questions.

Chapter 12
Aftermath

Ashley looked up at John, puzzled. "John, what's wrong?" He hadn't stepped on her toes, but something was throwing off his rhythm and timing.

He turned to her, looking a little confused. "I'm sorry. What did you say?"

"I asked you what was wrong."

"Oh, it's nothing. I thought I saw someone I used to know, but I was wrong."

"Hmm, you look like you've seen a ghost."

He snorted, "You're not far from wrong. The person I thought I saw is some who died a while ago. But like I said, I was wrong." He spun her around, and they faced the other direction.

Ashley could tell this wasn't the whole truth. He was trying to hide it, but something had obviously upset him.

Stephen managed to get Rose out of the building in time for her to throw up in a planter. He pulled out a handkerchief and carefully wiped her mouth. Tears streamed down her face, and she shook like a leaf.

"Rose, I won't let him hurt you. I won't let him come near you."

She buried her face in his shirt and cried harder. Stephen held her close, having no idea what he could do about the situation. He glanced around. They were on a public street and starting to draw attention. He got her moving and headed toward the parking garage. They made slow but steady progress, and eventually he had her seated in his car. She'd stopped crying, but she still shook. This wasn't doing her or the baby any good. Making up his mind, he put the car in gear and headed for St. Luke's hospital.

Richard had watched Stephen walk to his wife, who looked like she was in shock, and he was ready to make his excuses and go help when Hampton walked up.

"Good evening, gentlemen. Richard, I don't believe I know your acquaintances. Would you mind introducing me?" Hampton gave his used-car-salesman smile.

Richard wanted to belt the man. Obviously Bartlett had put two and two together and suspected that Richard had hired the data firm. Well, time to throw the wool over his eyes.

"Senator Hampton, allow me to introduce a new member of the house, Representative Paul Miller. And this is Mr. Miller's brother, Sam," Richard hoped and prayed that the two were quick on the uptake.

"Nice to meet you, Senator. I'm looking forward to working with you in the legislature this year." Paul Miller held out his hand.

Richard thanked his lucky stars that Paul was quick. The man would definitely be an asset on their team. While Hampton glad-handed everyone, he took the opportunity to glance over at Rose and make sure everything was all right. What he saw alarmed him even more. Rose was shaking and pointing at the dance floor, and Stephen turned the color of custard pudding.

What on earth was the matter? He followed the direction of their joint stares and saw a man dancing with Ashley who also was looking strange. Who was that man? Richard had never seen him before, but it was clear that Rose and Stephen knew him and he, them.

Hampton was pumping Paul and his brother for information, and the two men were evading his questions with considerable skill. Maybe it was time to turn the tables and get some information from the governor's weasel.

"Excuse me, Senator Hampton. Do you happen to know who that gentleman is dancing with Senator Halliday?" He pointed to the dance floor.

Hampton seemed annoyed at being interrupted but turned to look where Richard pointed. "Oh that's just one of the governor's staff. Now Mr. Miller, I understand your company is very good at data analysis, I was wondering…"

"Excuse me, Senator, but does the staffer have a name?" Richard kept a pleasant smile on his face.

Hampton gave him a scowl. "It's John Leeds. Now where was I before I got interrupted? Oh yes, analysis. I was wondering if you would be able to do some work for the governor."

"Well, he'd need to make an appointment and let us know what information he needs, and we'll see if we can help him and then proceed from there." Sam pulled a business card from his pocket and handed it to Hampton.

Richard had already lost interest in the conversation. He knew Miller's policy of confidentiality, and there was nothing he could do to stop him from taking the job if he wanted it. At the moment, he was more concerned about Rose and Stephen. They had both left the room, and Ashley was still dancing with John Leeds. Richard made a mental note to call Tomblin on Monday and add another name to his surveillance list.

Hampton, having evidently gotten what he came for, said his goodbyes and left the group. Richard watched him leave, and as soon as he was out of earshot, turned to the Millers. "Well, I don't know about you two, but I need a good stiff drink to wash the bad taste out of my mouth."

The Millers both laughed. "I completely agree," Sam said and led the way to the nearest liquor cart.

It took a while before Rose was examined by a doctor and admitted overnight for observation. The doctor had prescribed a mild sedative, and Rose fell asleep in the hospital bed, the monitor beeping with the rhythm of her steady heartbeat.

Stephen slouched in the chair beside her, his bowtie hanging loosely around his neck and his cummerbund draped over the arm of the chair. His tuxedo was getting wrinkled, but he really didn't have time to worry about that. How could John be standing in the flesh in this time? He clearly recognized Rose. What was he going to do with that knowledge? Stephen needed answers, and there was only one place to get them. That, however, was the problem. How did one summon an archangel?

He wracked his brain, but the only thing he could come up with was prayer. Should he get down on his knees or just bow his head where he sat? In the end, he decided to sit where he could see Rose, and he started to pray.

To his great relief, it didn't take long before a bright light appeared in the corner of his vision.

Gabriel's voice echoed in his mind. "I know what happened."

"How is it that John is walking around in the flesh? I mean, when you sent Rose to me, she was only able to communicate with me in dreams or through mirrors. How is it that John is solid?" Stephen kept his eyes averted from the light by watching Rose.

"Do you remember when I told you that someone was breaking the rules? Well, this is one of the rules being broken. Normally, when we use the spirit of someone who has died but is still in limbo, all they can do is appear in dreams or reflective surfaces. They are spirits, after all, and they communicate directly to the spirit or soul, if you will, in the living person. They cannot take physical form until they have fulfilled their assignment. Coming back to life is the reward for a job well done. One of the demons is breaking the rules by allowing John to take physical form when he needs to interact with people, but he can also speak to them through mirrors and in dreams like Rose did. I know that he has appeared that way to Ashley at least once."

Stephen fidgeted, rubbing his hands along his pants leg. "Do you think he is after Ashley?"

"I'm not really sure."

"How can you not know?"

"Stephen, have you ever played chess?"

"Yes, why?"

"Well, this is a lot like that game. I know what the ultimate goal of my opponent is, but I am not sure what path he plans to take to achieve it and which pieces he is willing to sacrifice to get there."

"Can he come after Rose?"

"Technically, no. Rose has already played her part and has received her reward. By the rules, she is to be left alone and allowed to live her new life. But as I said before, someone is breaking the rules. Now, if he plans to break this one, I don't know."

Stephen started to protest, but Gabriel interrupted him.

"I am keeping an eye on Rose and will protect her. I will not allow those who have served me be harmed by the others."

"What about Ashley? Can John hurt her?"

"That is possible, but you cannot warn her or anyone else. That rule is unbreakable," Gabriel said. "I'm afraid, for now, you must go on with your daily lives and simply watch things play out as they will."

Stephen wrung his hands. "That doesn't seem fair. I have to watch my friends be placed in danger, and I can't do anything about it."

"Remember, Stephen. Just because you are unable to warn them or help them does not mean that they are left defenseless. Now I must go; love your wife and treasure her. You and she have been given a great gift. Protect her and your son. I will be asking for your help in the future, but in the meantime, enjoy your blessings."

The light faded as Stephen whispered, "My son?"

Chapter 13
Speculations

John paced back and forth on his plot. If he had been solid instead of spirit, he'd have worn a foot-deep path through the center of the space.

Rose was alive and in this time. He still couldn't wrap his head around the fact. She'd died. His father had sent a telegram to Lewiston, where he was campaigning.

Argh. He shook his fist at the sky. Her death had destroyed his career. How could she be here now, and who was the man who escorted her out of the ballroom? He swung his fist at the tombstone. Why didn't Abaddon tell him?

John leaned back on his headstone and shook his head. He could see it all before him, everything in the past that had changed his life. He closed his eyes and remembered standing in his bedroom on the second floor of his parent's house staring out the window at the darkening sky. The meeting on statehood was planned more than a month ago. The territorial legislature wouldn't stop discussing it. The federal government had sent a representative from Washington to discuss the terms and procedures for joining the Union.

John was expected to attend with his wife to represent the mining interests of the family as well as his own political ambitions. Rose had a bad cold. She should have stayed in bed, but his mother had insisted that she be present. At breakfast, his mother announced that she had decided to attend as well, not trusting that he would handle things properly. He scowled. His mother always tried to run things. No wonder his father spent so much time inspecting the family's mining properties.

He shifted his position on the headstone. Everything was set to go in spite of the expected rainstorm. That's when Felicia's maid had arrived bearing a note. Her aunt Miriam was ill, and the doctor had prescribed laudanum to help her rest. Her aunt would be asleep for hours, so she could slip out of the house and see him. An evening's tryst with Felicia was far more preferable than going out in a storm to attend a boring political meeting, so he let it be known he had a terrible headache and wouldn't attend.

He could still see the look on Rose's face when he came downstairs with his mother, informing her he was staying home. Rose had looked like she wanted to cry. He felt a little pity for her, but she could rest after the meeting was over. He looked at her face. Her nose was red, and her cheeks looked flushed. Even sick, she was the most beautiful woman he had ever seen. She had pulled out a handkerchief and dabbed her nose again. His mother insisted that she go and represent him, sick or not.

By that time, the rainstorm was in full swing with gusting winds, thunder, and lightning. Felicia had arrived earlier, and he'd kept her hidden in his bedroom. Things would have been fine, if only Rose's doctor hadn't gone to the meeting. John still didn't know how the man had done it, but somehow he'd persuaded John's mother to allow Rose to go home. That's when she'd walked in on him and Felicia.

He should have locked his bedroom door. If he had, Rose would have gone to her own room and never been the wiser. But alas, he hadn't. He kicked at the headstone. Why couldn't Rose have stayed at the meeting? He started pacing again. After Rose found him in bed with Felicia, she'd left the house, running out into the storm in only a traveling cloak. John never saw her again.

He took a deep breath. He had told his father in the morning what had happened. His father wasn't happy about it but understood, having had a string of his own mistresses over the years. He advised John to take a trip to Lewiston and wait for things to blow over, which John had done immediately. His mother, upon hearing the news, invited Felicia to join her on a trip to Denver. Three days later, he got the telegram that Rose had died of pneumonia.

John ran his fingers through his hair. Things might have worked out if it wasn't for Rose's father. The man was so grief-stricken by the loss of his only child that he told anyone and everyone the details of what had happened. All the political support that his family had spent time and effort acquiring dried up and vanished. People gave him odd looks in the street. John found himself ostracized by most of the prominent Boise families, and soon the only women who would spend time with him were the whores at the brothel.

He shook his fists at the sky. "Why is she here?" he screamed.

Stephen sat in a chair beside Rose. She slept, getting much-needed rest. Stephen's chair wasn't the most comfortable. It was stiff and had cold, metal armrests. He tried leaning forward with his head resting on the bed, only to wake up a few minutes later with a stiff back. He did manage to doze for a time but was startled awake by a nurse coming in to check on Rose. After that, he gave up altogether and started thinking about what he could do to protect his wife and son. A son, he still couldn't believe it. His mind kept flashing images of a little boy learning to ride a bicycle, playing baseball, and smiling with ice cream smeared all over his face. A little boy, Peter Michael Winship, named after Rose's father and his own. He sat up straight in the chair. Nobody was going to hurt his family, not John, not Bartlett, not anyone.

Stephen got up and paced the room. The house was secure. He'd had a company install an alarm system along with video cameras and motion detectors when he and Rose were married. Rose's shop, however, was not safe. He made a mental note to call the same company on Monday and have them install a system at the dress shop as quickly as possible.

He sat back down beside the bed and stroked her hair. "I love you, Rose. I won't let anything happen to you."

Richard kept glancing around the bar. He had the most uncomfortable feeling he was being watched.

The bar was filled with the usual crowd watching various sporting events on the many televisions mounted on the walls or hanging from the ceiling. He sat in his favorite place at the corner of the bar, a spot that gave a good panoramic view of the room. He scanned the crowd, but no one seemed out of place or even paid the slightest attention to him. Still, the feeling would not go away. Richard pulled his phone out of his pocket and stared at it. With all the stories about the government being able to listen in on calls and keep track of people, perhaps he should pick up a burner phone for his conversations with Jason. He shook his head and picked up his drink. Maybe he was just being silly. He took a sip, and words he had heard once in a movie came to mind, something about the problem was not being paranoid but not being paranoid enough. He nodded. Yes, he would definitely pick up a burner phone. Richard raised his glass and drained it.

Abaddon stood in the corner of the bar staring at Richard Fowler. The man could sense him; that was clear. Odd, he wasn't one of the people Gabriel had used. Perhaps he was naturally sensitive to the supernatural. If that was the case, Richard could cause problems. He would need to keep track of this man.

"Ashley, can you pull the scalloped potatoes out of the oven and place them on the table?"

"Yes, Mom." Ashley got up from the sofa, leaving her two sisters-in-law chatting about their Christmas vacations. Her two brothers were with her dad in his game room. Ashley wondered why she always had to help Mom get things ready during these family dinners. Old stereotypes die hard.

Her mother was going all out for this family gathering. Probably to make up for running away to Hawaii for Christmas. "Ouch." She accidently touched a corner of the large casserole dish. *That's probably my punishment for thinking uncharitable thoughts.*

"Are you all right, dear?" Norma was busy tossing a salad by the sink.

"I'm fine. Is there anything else I can do?" Ashley carried the dish to the dining room.

"Can you put the rolls in the basket?" Norma set a large crystal bowl full of spinach and strawberries on the table.

The table looked elegant, decorated with fine china, crystal glasses, and polished silverware. Ashley smiled, thinking of Richard's dining table on Christmas Eve. She headed back in the kitchen and removed the rolls from their baking trays. She remembered dancing with him last night and how good it felt to be in his arms. She finished filling one basket and started on the second. This was silly, thinking about Richard like she was back in high school. She was nearly thirty, and she'd known Richard for at least two years. Still, things were different now. She flashed back to Christmas Eve and the progression of the evening. Her face grew warmer, and she nearly dropped the last roll.

"Ashley, is everything all right? You look a little flushed." Her mother came over and grabbed the first basket.

"I'm fine. I was just thinking."

Her mother raised an eyebrow. "About whom?"

Ashley straightened up, hastily grabbing the baking sheets and heading for the sink. This wasn't the time to tell her family about Richard. Not until she had everything worked out in her own mind. An alarm went off and interrupted her thoughts.

"Oh good, the turkey is ready." Her mother opened the oven and reached for the potholders.

One of Ashley's nephews wandered in to the kitchen. "I'm hungry; is it ready yet?"

"Yes, Willie. Go tell Grandpa that it's time to eat." Norma lifted out the golden brown bird and set it on the counter. "I just have to put it on the serving tray. Dad or one of the boys can carve it at the table."

Ashley nodded and picked up two bowls of steaming vegetables, walking them into the dining room.

The family came in from all directions and gathered at the two tables in the dining room. The adults at the large table and the children at the smaller one.

Her parents sat on either end of the table with her brothers and their wives on each of the sides and an extra chair for Ashley on the side by her mother. She flashed on the thought of Richard seated across from her and suppressed a smile. No sense bringing anyone's attention to the fact that she was alone. For now.

The children's table was a smaller version of the main dining table. The settings were similar, except the china was from an old set and cups were made of glass instead of Waterford crystal.

Her dad carved the turkey, and the rest of the family passed around the other plates, with her sisters-in-law scooping food out for the children. Ashley had three nephews and three nieces. Bill had two girls and a boy, and Tom had two boys and a girl.

Conversation around the table was pleasant, with everyone discussing their Christmas adventures. Ashley remained silent and listened politely. There was no way she was going to tell them about her Christmas experience. That brought Richard to mind again, and she picked up her wine glass and took a sip to cover up anything that might show on her face. She'd always been treated as the princess in the family, but something had changed last year. Maybe her family had never expected her to be elected a state senator. They were all friendly and supportive until after the election. She glanced around at her family. All the men were very successful in their fields, and all the women stayed at home. The thought struck her like a brick. Was that it? Was the princess supposed to marry a prince and start producing the heirs? That made her angry.

Her father spoke to her, but she didn't hear him the first time.

"I'm sorry, what did you say?"

"I asked if you did anything interesting over Christmas." He raised his fork and took a mouthful of potatoes.

"I made the short list for the lieutenant governor position."

A fork clattered to the floor.

Chapter 14
Answers

John felt Abaddon's approach, and his skin started to crawl. He closed his eyes and bit his lip. John wanted and needed answers, and as repulsive as he found this creature, it was the only one who could give them to him.

John ran his fingers through his hair. He still had no idea why the demon brought him back from the dead, but there had to be a reason. The cemetery was full of possible candidates. He'd seen them on various occasions. Lonely spirits staring out into the night, unable to leave or rest, tethered to the small plot of ground that held their bones. Abaddon had freed him, which meant he was chosen above the others. Abaddon needed him. Perhaps he could leverage this need and get the demon to provide some answers. He straightened up and tucked in his shirt, not knowing if this would help his case or not.

The dark figure came closer like a man on a casual stroll through a park. He stopped in front of John. The raspy voice echoed in John's mind. "I sense you have questions."

John stuttered. "I…ah…I want to know why Rose is here."

Abaddon laughed, a truly frightening sound. "You have a lot more questions than that. You want to know why I chose you and what your purpose is here." He paused for a moment. "You're here because Rose is here."

John started with surprise. "What?"

"I'm not in the habit of repeating myself."

"But I don't understand."

"You don't have to. You only have to do what I tell you to do."

John bent his head and stared at the ground. "Please."

Abaddon laughed again, and John stuffed his fingers in his ears.

Abaddon walked around the gravesite and stopped beside the headstone. "Perhaps you should know." A bony hand protruded from the sleeve of his robe and stroked the stone. "Have you ever read the Bible?"

John backed up to the limit of his plot. "Yes, well parts of it anyway. Why?"

"Ever read Ephesians 6:12?"

John shook his head.

"For our struggle is not against flesh and blood, but against the rulers, against the powers, against the world forces of this darkness, against the spiritual forces of wickedness in the heavenly places," Abaddon quoted.

John stared at Abaddon, confused.

As fast as a bolt of lightning, Abaddon's hand struck him in the head, and he fell to the ground.

It took a few minutes before John's head cleared and he could think straight again. He lay on the cold wooden floor of the foyer of a house. A woman walked in carrying a mop and bucket. She looked familiar. It took a moment to place her. Molly, his mother's Irish housemaid.

"Molly, help me."

The woman ignored him and set her bucket down. A little water slopped over the sides.

"Molly, I told you to help me."

She put her mop in the bucket and wrung some of the water out before starting to clean the floor.

"Bloody useless servant." John got slowly to his feet. "Molly," he screamed.

The maid kept on cleaning.

John stomped over to her and tried to slap her face. His hand passed right through her, and a jolt ran up his arm that almost stopped his heart.

He shook his tingling fingers. Of course, he was dead. This wasn't real. It was like the dreams he gave to Ashley, a memory.

Only this wasn't anything he remembered. Could it be Abaddon's memory? The thought sent a shock through him greater than the one he had just experienced.

Abaddon was a demon; perhaps he could simply show scenes from the past without having actually witnessed them. He shook his head to clear it. What day was it, and why did Abaddon want him to see this particular one? Surely it had to contain something more interesting than watching the maid clean the foyer. As if on cue, someone pounded on the front door.

Molly looked shocked and dropped her mop. She looked around, apparently hoping someone else would come in and deal with the unexpected visitor. She gave a small whine and walked over to the door.

The visitor continued pounding and shouting. It sounded to John like a foreign language. He frowned. That didn't make the slightest bit of sense.

Molly straightened her cap and ran her hands down her sides to smooth her apron and then carefully opened the door. A small gray-haired man with steel-rimmed spectacles came in.

"Where is John Leeds?" He managed to say in the midst of a lot of other words John couldn't understand.

John walked closer to the man. His hair was disheveled and tear tracks were clearly visible on his cheeks. It took another moment, but then it hit him like a hammer. This was Peter Van Buren, Rose's father. He'd only seen the man a few times. What was he doing here?

"Where is John Leeds?" the old man shouted again.

The sound of a door closing upstairs drew everyone's attention to the staircase. John's father came down the steps, fastening the sash belt of his morning coat.

"I'm John Leeds," his father answered.

"Not you. I want your son," the old man said, his face turning scarlet with anger.

"He isn't here. He left for Lewiston two days ago."

That seemed to completely enrage the old man. He screamed in his own tongue at John's father. John belatedly remembered that the Van Burens had come from Holland. In the long string of foreign words, the few he caught and understood were coward, beautiful child, and dead.

"Oh, sweet Lord, this must be the morning that Rose died." John ran his fingers through his hair.

John's father stepped forward. "Sir, you must calm down and explain to me what has happened. Come into the parlor." He stretched out a hand toward the door on the left. "Molly, tell the butler to bring in some brandy and two glasses. Come, sir, this way please."

Peter closed his eyes and took a deep breath in a visible effort to control himself. After a few minutes, he opened his eyes and nodded, and then followed John's father into the parlor.

The room was large, with a huge, stone fireplace in the center of the outside wall. Several wingback chairs stood scattered about room, each with a small end table beside it. The windows were all covered with heavy drapes.

His father stepped into the room just ahead of the butler carrying a tray, and he walked to a chair in front of the fireplace and sat down. He motioned to Peter to take a seat close to him. The butler placed a glass at each table, poured a generous amount of brandy for both men, and left the decanter beside his employer. He moved about the room, opening the drapes and lighting some lamps.

John watched Peter take a gulp from his glass. The old man barely held his emotions in check.

His father and his guest remained silent while the butler worked.

John paced the room, waiting for Peter to notice the paintings on the wall. One of the Leeds's family traditions was to have a portrait done of each family member as they were added. The portraits were updated with spouses and grandchildren as the children grew.

A large portrait of his mother hung over the fireplace, glowering into the room. John rolled his eyes; it was an appropriate place considering how his mother ran the entire household. On the right hung one of his father, painted some fifteen years ago. On the left hung John's portrait, done two years ago. On another wall were his oldest sister, Caroline, and her husband the carriage maker, along with their two children. On the opposite wall was his other sister, Annabelle, with her husband the shipping mogul and their three children. On the back wall all by itself was the portrait of Rose, done six months ago.

John felt a pang of sorrow looking at her beautiful face and knowing she had died. He took a step towards the picture just as Peter saw it. A mournful cry escaped his lips, and he rose stiffly from his chair. He went and stood in front of it, tears flowing down his face as he raised his hand toward the picture.

John's father had turned in his chair to watch, brandy forgotten on the table. "I'm sorry. When did it happen?"

Peter choked out, "Early...this morning."

John's father stood up and walked over to the portrait. "I am sorry. I know what my son did. I wish the boy had more sense. I loved Rose. She was truly a jewel, and my son did not have the wit or maturity to see that. I know there is nothing I can do to ease your grief, but I want to give you this painting of her. We are not worthy of having it hanging on our wall." He walked over to a bell cord and pulled it. The butler came in a moment later.

"Take down this picture of Rose and have it sent to Mr. Van Buren's home as soon as possible." He turned to the old man. "Can I help with the arrangements for her final resting place?"

Peter wiped his face with his sleeve. "No. I will bury her myself. I thank you for the picture, but I will never forgive your son or your family for how they treated her." He took one last look at the portrait, and then he turned on his heel and walked out of the house.

John was watching the old man leave when everything began to blur. A few moments later, he stood in the back of a small room with several men who were sitting around a table drinking and smoking cigars.

John shook his head. Obviously, Abaddon had something else he wanted John to see. Very well then, where was he? He glanced around the room. It looked vaguely familiar. He wandered over to one of the windows and looked out onto Main Street. Of course, this was the private room above Porter's Saloon. He went back to the table and examined the faces of all of the people gathered there. He recognized the six men as members of the mining consortium and the two whores from Madam Bella's establishment.

They were drinking good whiskey; John could smell it. By all rights, he should have been included in this group as his family's representative. Was this after he had died?

The leader of the group, an Irishman named Gary Sullivan, got up and tapped a cigar clipper against his glass.

"Gentlemen, we are all in agreement that statehood for Idaho at this time is detrimental to our various business interests. Most of the members of the territorial legislature want it to happen by the summer of next year. We have to find someone to represent our interests and lobby the legislature. It must be someone who appears to be respectable but is willing to do anything and everything to get statehood delayed." He stopped and took a drink of his whiskey.

"Gary, are we talking about bribery?" asked an overweight man who had one of the whores on his lap.

"We are talking bribery, persuasion, and blackmail, whatever it takes." Sullivan puffed his cigar.

Another man spoke up. "Well, the best person for the job isn't in the room. I think we should use John Leeds. Not the old man but the son. Little Johnny has the morals of an alley cat and no scruples to speak of. He's perfect."

There was a general murmur of approval from the group.

A large man on the other side of the table picked up his glass. "Are we sure we can trust him? A man with no principles can be bought and sold by anyone. Besides I hear he's a bit of a drunk."

That brought general laughter.

John stood, stunned. He remembered quite well when Sullivan approached him with the offer to be the group's representative. Sullivan told him that his past political experience was invaluable, and that, combined with his knowledge of the mining industry and its needs, well, that made him the ideal candidate.

He scowled. So that was what they really thought of him. He'd been under the impression that he was discrete with his visits to the brothels, and as for drinking, well everyone drank too much.

The room started to shimmer, and he grabbed the back of a chair to steady himself. A moment later he stood in the Van Buren's dry goods store.

Peter was helping a customer with the purchase of a shovel while his assistant was busy helping a lady load her purchases into a wagon. The store looked much as he remembered it, except for one thing. Rose was not there.

He remembered the first time he'd seen her. His mother was buying some material to have a dress made for the party to celebrate his graduation from Harvard. Rose pulled out different bolts of cloth from a wall rack while his mother inspected the material and held it up against the lace she was using to trim her gown.

The thought of Rose still took his breath away, her long honey-colored hair, her sweet angelic face. He'd wanted her from the moment he saw her. The perfect prop to have on his arm for the race to be governor of a new state. The complements he'd gotten about her and the stares of envy from other men only increased his desire. She was exactly what he wanted, and she destroyed him.

Peter finished with his customer and went back to the counter. He grabbed a pitcher and poured some water into a cup. Another man walked into the store; John recognized him as a member of the territorial legislature.

"Peter, I need a new bucket. What do you have in stock?"

Peter led the man to the far side of the store where a small collection of buckets in three different sizes was stacked.

"Which size did you need?"

The man looked around and lowered his voice. "Actually, I don't need one. I wanted to have a quiet word with you without anybody being suspicious.

Peter raised his eyebrows. "What is the matter, Joseph?"

"I just came from Porter's Saloon, where I heard something you might be interested in."

"Oh." Peter frowned. "Does it have to do with the Leeds family?"

"Yes it does. Peggy, one of the…ah…ladies from Madam Bella's establishment was there to pick up some refreshments for their customers, and she told me what the mining consortium plans to do for John, the son."

Peter stiffened.

Joseph took a few minutes to detail what the whore had told him. Peter's face grew redder as the other man spoke. At the end, Peter nodded. "Thank you for telling me."

The other man nodded and picked up a small bucket. "I'll take this one. My wife could use a new bucket for her garden."

John scratched his head. Why was Abaddon showing him this? Rose's father knew about the consortium's plans, but what difference did that make? He didn't remember anyone talking about the plan. The last he remembered, things were well underway. He'd received the appointment as the group's representative–lobbyist would have been a better term–but he'd started the job and had already persuaded five of the legislators to change their vote on statehood before he was killed.

The room started to shimmer again, and he grabbed onto a shelf. When things came back into focus, he stood in a small sitting room. One glance at the portrait of Rose on the wall told him he was in Peter's living quarters. Peter sat on a sofa in front of a small table. On the table, five candles burned around a small bowl filled with leaves. John sniffed the air. It was sage. Peter spoke in his native language, but John could tell he was reciting some type of prayer. None of this made any sense to him, and he backed away from the strange old man.

The room shimmered, and he found himself standing outside of Porter's Saloon. The door opened, and he saw himself stagger out holding a bottle of whiskey. "Oh Lord, this is the night I died."

He walked carefully behind his living self, checking from side to side for the one who killed him. He was about halfway home when he passed a large wooded lot at the edge of the city that marked the entrance to Warm Springs Road where his parents' house stood. His living self walked past a large lilac bush, and a man stepped out from behind it. John recognized Peter, and he was holding a knife. What? Rose's father was the man who killed him?

He watched in horror as the old man took the knife and jabbed it in John's back, just under the ribs. John watched his body fall and the whiskey bottle break on the ground. Peter pulled the knife out and blood spread from John's coat onto the dirt.

The stab wound pained John, and he grabbed his side as the world went black.

John woke up lying on the ground while Abaddon still leaned on the headstone. The demon's raspy voice echoed in his mind. "Now you see what led to your death."

John shook his head trying to clear it. "I can see what happened, but it still doesn't explain why Rose is here."

"Do you remember Peter praying with the candles and burning sage?"

John nodded.

"Peter is from the old country and was taught the old ways. He and others like him have heard from childhood the stories about angels and demons and how they manipulate the affairs of men. Peter wasn't praying, he was offering a deal."

John stared. "What deal?"

"Statehood is a big issue, and he knew it would be important to someone. It was. An angel took his deal. Your death for a second chance at life for his daughter."

Abaddon moved away from the headstone and walked around the plot. "Peter was willing to sacrifice himself by committing a great sin to save his daughter. Rose, in turn, was asked to fulfill an assignment for the angel. She did. This is the result."

Abaddon raised his hand and struck John again, and he fell to the ground. A series of images flashed before his eyes. Rose in the arms of the man at the ball. The man slowly removing her dress, kissing her after he unfastened each button. The same man standing beside her in a church, obviously at their wedding, and the two of them laughing.

The visions stopped, and John slowly got to his feet. "Who is this man?"

"His name is Stephen Winship, and he's her husband. He was supposed to marry Ashley Halliday until he met Rose."

John clenched his fists.

"Rose is carrying his child. They are going to have a son."

John closed his eyes and snarled. This was so unfair. He had treated Rose badly, but it was her own stupidity that had sent her out in that storm with a bad cold. If she had just accepted his affair with Felicia, everything would have been fine. His mother knew about all his father's mistresses and never made a fuss. His mother just accepted things as they were. Why couldn't Rose have done the same? Anger kept building inside of him.

"Have I answered your questions?"

"Yes, thank you."

With that, Abaddon vanished.

John paced his burial plot. It wasn't right that Rose should have a new life while he languished in the spirit world. True, Abaddon had promised him another chance at life, but could he really trust a demon to keep his word? He ran his fingers through his hair. Rose had recognized him, and he was sure she'd told her husband about him. Husband. John spat out the word. Rose belonged to him and no one else. He'd make them both pay for what had happened to him. Now, how to do it? He paced some more. Getting to Rose was out of the question. Winship would protect her. The best thing to do was come at them from an angle they didn't expect. That angle was Ashley. She obviously meant something to Fowler, and Fowler was Winship's best friend. John stopped in front of his headstone. He'd do as Abaddon asked and flirt with the governor's daughter, but it was Ashley he intended to seduce and use against Rose and Winship.

Abaddon stood a few yards away listening to John's little plans. He laughed to himself. The fool thought he could hide his intentions. No matter; John's plan to seduce Ashley worked well with his own goals. Gabriel wanted Winship to win the governor's race. Abaddon wanted someone else. If John tried seducing and corrupting Ashley, it might cause Winship or Rose to try to warn her. If they told anyone else the truth of what and who John was or that supernatural power was involved, Rose would be sent back to limbo, permanently stuck there. Winship would be distraught by the loss of his wife and possibly his son, if they warned Ashley before the child was born. Winship would drop out of the governor's race, and Gabriel's plans would be thwarted. Abaddon

102

smiled. And John, the stupid fool, would lose his second chance at life for not doing exactly as he was told. Abaddon couldn't see a downside to this. He grinned widely, revealing his fangs. It looked like he would win this game against Gabriel after all.

Chapter 15
The Session Begins

Ashley walked into the senate chamber and looked for her place.
Each desk had the name of the senator and the district he or she
represented listed on a plaque. The first meeting was largely
ceremonial. Members of the senate were sent to the house and the
governor to inform both that the senate was ready to begin work.
Likewise, members of the house and the governor's staff came to
the senate to report the same. All of this was steeped in history and
tradition. Ashley smiled and twitched with excitement. At the
conclusion of these formalities, all the senators marched across the
rotunda to the house chamber. Because there were seventy
members of the house and thirty-five members of the senate, the
house chamber was larger.

Chairs were set up in the well of the house for each of the
senators, the judges of the supreme court and the district courts,
and the constitutional officers. Ashley saw Richard as she headed
toward her seat. He gave her a big smile. Stephen's desk was two
rows down from Richard's. Stephen gave her a nod as she passed.

When everyone was seated, Governor Russell James Bartlett
entered the chamber like a king getting ready to address his
subjects. Ashley wanted to roll her eyes, but there were too many
people around, and showing disrespect for the governor was not a
good idea for a freshman senator.

People stood and applauded Bartlett, and Ashley was obliged
to stand as well. Looking around, it dawned on her that every state-
level elected official was in this room.

The gallery above them was full of visitors, and, of course, the
media was present. Bartlett walked up to the podium, and people in

the room began to settle down. He cleared his throat and started reading his prepared speech from the teleprompter.

Ashley found a comfortable position; members were expected to pay attention and applaud at statements and programs they agreed with.

Bartlett praised the state, speaking about its citizens, beauty, natural resources, industry, and technology. He continued by talking about all the programs he had introduced during his time in office.

Ashley wondered if Stephen was taking notes, so he could counter all these claims when he announced his candidacy. Actually there was no need; cameras recorded the entire event, and the video would be available online for anyone to watch or analyze it. Mandy would take care of that. No doubt they already had a pretty good idea what Bartlett would talk about and had Stephen's speech prepared. Still, the old fox could throw in some new ideas or proposals that no one had anticipated. She carefully shifted her position. Bartlett clearly enjoyed being center stage and was making the most of it. She could tell by his speech pattern that he was just warming up, and this would be a long one. If only she could turn around and see Richard's and Stephen's reactions to the yarns the governor was spinning. Unfortunately, her movements would be too noticeable. She didn't want to insult or alienate the man; after all, Bartlett still hadn't made his choice for lieutenant governor.

Stephen wanted to be almost anywhere but here, listening to that blowhard brag about what a wonderful job he'd been doing. If his words were manure, they'd have had to clean out the house chamber with a backhoe. He shifted in his chair. Thank heavens the doctor had ordered Rose to stay home today. The thought of John appearing in her shop made him feel like he had missed a step walking downstairs. The security company he'd called this morning could start work tomorrow. There'd be workmen in and out of the shop for several days. She'd be safe with all those witnesses, and once the system was installed, there would be surveillance in the common areas and a panic room. It was expensive, but he couldn't put a price on Rose's safety.

He wished Bartlett would hurry up and finish, so he could head home and see his wife. In the meantime, all he could do was sit quietly and look like he was deeply absorbed in the speech.

Richard wondered what would happen if he just got up and left the room. Bartlett was hitting his stride, and it was obvious they'd be stuck here for an hour or more. It wouldn't be so bad if he could at least text Stephen during this torture, but the Speaker had strictly forbidden the use of cell phones today. He sighed. That was probably just as well. The irreverent comments they'd be sending back and forth would have them each sustaining an injury with the effort not to laugh.

Bartlett kept moving, addressing specific points to different sides of the room. Richard took advantage of Bartlett's eyes being focused elsewhere to glance around the room and up into the visitor's gallery. The room was completely packed. Good thing the air conditioning was working. Movement in the upper gallery caught his eye, and he saw John Leeds from the governor's office come in and lean against the wall. Richard's fists tightened. The man was clearly staring at Ashley and in a manner Richard didn't like. At least he'd called Jason this morning and left a message to add Leeds to his surveillance list. Something wasn't right about the guy, but he couldn't put his finger on what it was.

When Bartlett turned his gaze to Richard's side of the room, he had to pay attention again. Hopefully, he wouldn't fall asleep and start snoring before the old windbag finally shut up.

John looked around the room. It was a far cry from the original meeting places of the territorial legislature. It reminded him of the capitol building in Washington. He had been able to visit it several times while he was going to school. He found Ashley almost immediately. She had her hair done up and wore a deep-blue jacket over a short but flattering white dress. She had to be the youngest member of the senate by at least fifteen years. When the speech was over, she'd probably use the main exit, considering she was seated pretty close to it. If he hurried, he could go out the back way and meet her on the third floor of the rotunda between the two staircases. Perhaps he could talk her into having lunch with him in the cafeteria in the basement. The governor kept an account there that the staff could use. He continued to watch her. It didn't really matter if they went to lunch as long as he could talk to her for a while.

Bartlett didn't sound like he was coming near the end, but it would probably be a good idea to start moving now to make sure he didn't miss Ashley leaving. John was just about to move when he spotted him, Rose's husband. He curled his fists and wanted to hit something. Rose was his wife first, and no one took from him something that was his. His eyes narrowed. He'd make them pay, both of them and anyone who was associated with them.

He glanced back to Ashley. She was his way to get to Rose. He wasn't sure how he'd do it, but he'd take away Rose's new life as payment for what her father had done to him. Two can play at this game of revenge, and if the pretty senator got torn up in the process, well, so be it. John turned and quietly slipped back out of the room.

He made it all the way out to the walkway when he ran into the governor's private secretary.

"Oh, there you are. How is the speech going?"

John gave her a smile to cover up his irritation. "I only heard part of it, but it sounded good."

"Does it look like the legislature is receiving it well?"

"I couldn't tell. Everyone appeared to be listening with interest, and I did hear them clap in the right places, but you never know for sure."

She frowned. "That's true. Oh, Mason is looking for you. He wants you back in the office as soon as the speech is over."

"Can it wait a bit? I wanted to talk to someone after the speech."

"I don't think so. He seemed quite insistent."

"Oh, they're coming out. I'll meet you back at the office," John said.

The secretary turned and headed for the stairs.

What could the bloody man want now? Maybe he could have a short talk with Ashley and make plans for a longer meeting a little later. He had extra time today. Abaddon had given him until nine to return to his grave.

People came out of the main entrance, and he scanned the crowd for Ashley. It was hard to see through the knots of people. He kept looking for her blue jacket. The crowd started to thin, and he still hadn't spotted her. Could she have taken the back way or perhaps one of the elevators?

He went to the railing and looked down at the first floor of the capitol rotunda. There she was, talking to Fowler and walking toward the front doors.

Ashley slipped on her gloves as she walked. "Thanks for keeping my coat and things in your cloakroom. I really didn't want to go all the way back to my office in the senate wing."

"No problem; glad to be of service." Richard held the door open for her. A cold blast of January air hit them both in the face.

"Yuck, it feels like we're going to get more snow." Ashley pulled up her collar.

"The weatherman said we wouldn't have snow until tomorrow; of course, that means we're going to get buried tonight. Do you want me to fetch my car and drive us over?"

"No, I'll be warm enough once we start walking. I hope your bar has something hot for lunch. I'd love a bowl of soup."

Richard laughed. "We serve two kinds of soup daily during the winter months. One cream-based and one broth."

"That sounds delicious."

They kept the small talk to a minimum because of the cold.

Richard's bar was only three blocks from the capitol. Ashley's nose was pink. She could see her reflection in the large mirror over the bar. Richard took her coat and gloves and led her to a table in the corner.

A waitress came over and took away the "Reserved" sign. "What can I get you started with, boss?"

"Ashley?" Richard pulled out her chair.

She sat down, enjoying his good manners. "Can you make me a coffee mocha? I'd really like something hot to drink after that walk."

"Sure can, miss, and the usual for you, boss?"

"Yes, thanks, Misty. Bring us a couple of menus, please. And what are the soups today?"

"Loaded potato and old-fashioned chicken noodle," she said as she headed to the bar to get them their drinks.

Richard seated himself across from Ashley. "Which soup would you like?"

"I'll take the chicken. I love loaded potato, but it's too many calories."

Richard grinned. "You should compromise. Have a bowl of the chicken and a cup of the potato. I really want you to try the potato; it's my grandmother's recipe."

Ashley laughed. "All right, you win."

The waitress returned with their drinks.

"Wow, that was fast." Ashley sipped her coffee and closed her eyes. "I think my face is thawing out."

Richard drank some of his whiskey.

Ashley opened one eye. "Isn't it a little early to start drinking?"

Richard drank some more. "Not really, it's after five in Scotland, and this is good Scotch whisky. Besides, after having to listen to all that bull crap the governor was spewing, I could use a good drink."

"I couldn't believe it when he actually praised the federal Enhanced Education Program, and those idiots clapped. Don't they know what it will do to education in this state?" Ashley took another sip of her coffee.

"I think all they heard was the part about more grant dollars. It is amazing how many of them think it's free money. The federal government is a lot like a drug dealer; they give the states a new program and a taste of money to get them to accept it. By the time they are hooked, the grants dry up and they have a new entitlement they have to fund." Richard took another sip.

The waitress came back and took their order. More people entered the bar, and the place started to fill up.

Ashley bit her lip. "Richard, do any of Bartlett's staff ever come in here?"

He laughed. "They did up until Stephen introduced the grocery tax bill last year. I think he sent out a memo after that saying the place was off limits because I haven't seen any of his people since." He tilted his chin and studied her face. "I know you don't want to do anything that might hurt your chances at the lieutenant governor's position. I don't think having lunch here today will make any difference in his decision."

Ashley's cheeks grew warm. "I don't want to insult you, but I don't think it's a good idea for me to be seen talking to you at the capitol until he has made his decision."

Richard finished his drink and set the glass down. "You won't have time to talk to me for the next three weeks at least."

Ashley frowned. "What do you mean?"

"The session really starts tomorrow; you'll have your first committee meetings, and the business will really get started. Between all the bills you need to read, the issues you need to study, and the lobbyists who will be wining and dining you for your vote, you'll barely have time to catch your breath, let alone have a good conversation with friends."

The waitress returned, bringing them each a bowl of soup. It took her a second trip to bring Ashley's salad and cup of potato soup as well as Richard's club sandwich. They ate in companionable silence.

Ashley couldn't help thinking about the last meal they'd shared and the...ah...dessert that followed. Her cheeks grew hot again.

Richard set down his sandwich. "Is there too much pepper in the soup?"

Ashley hurriedly picked up a napkin and dabbed her lips.

Richard straightened up in his chair. "Ashley, I have an excellent memory, too." He leaned forward and looked into her eyes. "Let's do this thing right. Bartlett will make his decision by the end of January. In the meantime, we are both going to be very busy." He reached across the table and took her hand. "On the first Friday in February, go out with me on a date. Your choice of dinner and a movie, concert, play, or whatever you'd like to do." He stroked her palm with his thumb. "There is feeling between us, and I don't want to ignore it or push it away."

Ashley smiled and gave his hand a squeeze. "I'll let you know where we're going."

Chapter 16
Politics

John positioned himself near the entryway of the senate chamber. After yesterday's disaster, he wasn't leaving anything to chance. He glanced at the doors. The senate should be adjourning at any moment. He only had an hour for lunch, but he planned to make the most of it.

The doors opened and two pages came out, one headed for the stairs and the other for the rotunda. John cracked his knuckles. He wanted a pocket watch or maybe one of the modern watches that men wore on their wrists, but Abaddon wouldn't allow it. He didn't understand why; he'd asked once and only gotten a growl for an answer.

Two other men came up the stairs and stood on the opposite side of the entryway. Both were well-dressed and wore the green nametags that identified them as lobbyists. The doors opened again, and this time some of the members of the senate came out. He watched, shifting his weight from foot to foot, and spotted her coming through the doors talking to an elderly senator. John ran his fingers through his hair. The best approach was to keep it formal. Several people knew he was associated with Bartlett's office; if he made it appear he was doing something official for the governor, he'd be able to get her away and have a private conversation.

When Ashley got within four feet of him, he spoke. "Senator Halliday."

She turned. "John, how nice to see you."

"I was wondering if…"

"Ashley." The elderly senator called to her, and she turned away.

"These are the two men from the dairy industry that I told you about. Gentlemen, this is Senator Ashley Halliday."

The men immediately introduced themselves and led her and the elderly senator down the stairs. Ashley glanced back once and mouthed, "Sorry." John clenched his fists so tight, his knuckles turned white.

"John?" Rachel had come up behind him while he watched Ashley.

He took a second to compose his face before turning. "Hello, Rachel. Can I help you with something?"

"Well," she glanced down at her shoes. "Mason told me there is a cafeteria here, and that my dad's office keeps an account for the staff. I'm hungry, but I don't know where it is."

John gave her a smile; he might as well do something for Abaddon since his own plans turned out to be a bust. "I was getting ready to go there myself. Would you like some company for lunch?"

She gave him a warm smile. "Thank you. I'd like that."

Stephen sat down at his desk and pulled out his cell phone. He had a few minutes before he had to go to a lunch meeting with Richard and the rest of their land-bill group. All morning long, he kept thinking of Rose and wondering how far the workmen had gotten. He turned on his phone and watched all the messages appear on the screen. None appeared to be urgent; he'd call them back after the afternoon session was over. Right now, he wanted to talk to Rose.

Clair answered the phone, as usual.

Rose still wasn't comfortable with the device. He heard the sounds of hammering and a drill while he waited for Rose to come to the phone.

"Hello?"

"Hi, sweetheart, how is the construction going?"

"It's rather noisy, but they seem to be making good progress. Mr. Bowman says the alarm system will be finished by Friday and the special room will take another two weeks." A power saw sounded in the background.

"How are you feeling?"

"I'm all right. Clair is here, and there are lots of other people around. I'm just worried about having to wait for the bus." There was a slight quiver in her voice.

"Don't worry about that. I have made arrangements with a private taxi company. They will pick you up at the house and drive you to the shop. They'll be at the shop each evening at five thirty to take you home. All you'll have to do is walk out of the door and get into the car." Stephen heard voices coming down the hall. "I need to get going; I have a meeting. If you need anything or you feel uncomfortable, call the special number I gave you. I told the sergeant at arms that you're expecting, and if you call, they are to pull me out of whatever meeting or session I'm in."

"Okay. I love you."

"I love you too, sweetheart. I'll see you at home tonight. Bye." He hung up the phone.

"There you are. I had lunch brought in from the bar. Have you seen the others yet?" Richard came up to Stephen's desk with two pages behind him, each carrying a large box.

"No, where are we meeting?" Stephen set his phone down and reached for his briefcase.

"In the small meeting room down the hall. Are you ready?"

"Yes." Stephen stood up and followed.

Richard pulled a key out of his pocket and unlocked the conference room door. "Set the boxes down on the table."

The two pages moved past him and set their burdens down, both looking rather relieved.

Richard reached into his coat pocket, pulled out two twenties, and handed one to each young man. "Here, get yourselves some lunch."

"Thank you, Mr. Fowler," said the tall one with the bad acne.

"Yes, thank you, sir," his fellow chimed in.

"You're welcome."

The two left the room. Richard stood in the doorway, waiting until they were out of earshot. "I've invited Paul Miller to join us.

We might as well get him bloodied early, so he understands the uphill fight we have before us to get this bill passed."

Stephen chuckled. "Baptism by fire, huh. The poor guy may not want to run for reelection."

Richard grinned. "It's better to learn early what this is all about. It may be that he's not cut out for the work. At least we'll know quickly." He looked over Stephen's shoulder. "Oh good, here they come."

Marion and Frank came around the corner with Paul in tow.

When everyone was in the room, Richard locked the door.

"The food smells great, Richard," Marion said as she started unpacking containers. After a few minutes, they were all seated, nibbling on sandwiches and salad or sipping soup.

Richard set down his spoon. "Marion, pass me a bottle of water. Thanks. Okay, I wanted to bring everyone up to speed on where we are with the land bill."

The others shifted into positions that were more comfortable.

"As you know, the company doing our data mining and analysis is owned by Paul and his brother. The work is nearly complete. Paul says we will have the report in another two weeks." He glanced at Paul, who nodded. "Right now, I plan to introduce the bill in the State Affairs Committee on February first. The chairman knows I have a special bill coming; he does not know what it's about. I promised to let him know the Friday before, so he's prepared. He knows me pretty well, so he is expecting something big, and he won't be disappointed."

Frank grabbed a napkin and wiped his mouth. "How do you plan to make the case for the bill?"

"By the time the committee goes through the full report, the bill will be the obvious course of action to solve the problem." Richard took a sip from his bottle.

Marion shifted in her seat. "Is Ashley still going to be the senate sponsor?"

"That depends on what Bartlett does. If she's named lieutenant governor, then Senator Bellmore will sponsor the bill." Richard picked up his spoon.

Stephen spoke. "I know Ashley really wants the position, but Bartlett isn't going to name her. Mark my words; he's going to pick someone he can control who will be the point man for his agenda."

Richard nodded. "I know, but we need to let it play out."

Frank cleared his throat. "While we're waiting for Richard's land bill, I have a bill of my own to introduce. Since Bartlett wants to get the state entangled in the federal Enhanced Education Plan, I'm introducing a bill that will stop the loss of local control over education. The bill requires that each individual school board vote on acceptance of any curriculum used in their schools. This stops Bartlett from pushing things through the state Board of Education and having them dictate to all the individual school districts." Frank picked up his bottle of water and took a sip.

Richard nodded. "Well done, Frank. I take it you had help with this."

"I consulted with legislators in others states who turned down the program and found out how it was done. Three states used this type of legislation to defeat it. I had private attorneys look at the bill and make sure it would pass the state's constitutional muster, and it's ready to go. I am presenting it in the Education Committee next week." Frank grinned and looked rather pleased with himself.

"Great job; your bill and my land bill will stick a cork in the governor's plan." Richard turned to Paul. "You've been rather quiet."

"I'm trying to take it all in. I'm just beginning to realize how unprepared I am for all of this."

Marion laughed. "That is the first step to becoming a good legislator, realizing how much you don't know."

Richard checked his watch. "We should finish our lunches and head upstairs. We'll do this again next week and see where we are with Frank's bill and mine. Of course that also assumes that the smoke has cleared after your announcement that you're running for governor." He turned to Stephen.

"I wouldn't bet on that." Stephen set his fork down. "I will be announcing on Thursday instead of tomorrow."

Richard raised his eyebrows. "Oh, why's that?"

"Mandy checked the weather forecast, and it's supposed to snow tomorrow morning but clear up around three. If I wait until Thursday, it will give the capitol groundskeepers enough time to get the snow off the steps before we hold a rally there. Because I can't electioneer inside the capitol, I have to hold the rally outside the building. I need a lot of people for a show of support; I can't ask them to stand there in a snowstorm. I mean, they are already coming out in freezing weather."

"Mandy is very good at her job." Marion said.

"She's the best. She's had volunteers calling people and asking them to turn out. With any luck, we'll have a very respectable showing." Stephen picked up his half-eaten sandwich.

"Has she arranged security as well? After you officially announce, Bartlett will have the long knives out for you." Richard motioned with his fork.

"I'm not afraid of Bartlett, but that doesn't mean you're wrong. Mandy did arrange to have a few private security people scattered through the crowd just in case Bartlett tries a stunt like he pulled against his opponent three years ago." Stephen took another bite of his sandwich.

Paul looked confused. "What did he do?"

Richard wiped his mouth with a napkin. "He arranged to have some protesters at the man's announcement. They shouted at him, chanted slogans, and generally disrupted the gathering. The news reporters, of course, were more interested in the protest then the candidate, and it knocked his campaign off the rails before it even got started."

Marion glanced at her watch. "Oh, we need to get going. I promised Paul a quick lesson on house protocol. We have to meet the majority whip and borrow his book." She wiped her mouth on a napkin. "Thank you for lunch, Richard. It was delicious."

"You're welcome, Marion. We'll have it again at next week's meeting."

Frank rose as well. "I'd better get going, too. I have some phone calls to make before the session starts. Thanks, Richard."

The three left the room, and Richard took another sip from his water bottle.

"Stephen, I wanted to have a private chat with you about Ashley."

Stephen set his sandwich down and grinned. "Is this the part where you ask my permission to date my ex?"

Richard coughed. "You know?"

Stephen leaned back in his chair. "Richard, I've known you for five years. I've seen you with women before; you think I wouldn't notice the spark between you and Ashley?"

Richard scratched his chin. "And I was thinking I was both subtle and clever."

Stephen laughed. "I don't think anyone else noticed."

"So you're okay with it?"

Stephen took a sip from his water bottle before speaking. "I still feel bad about the way things went with Ashley. I thought she was something she isn't, and I never realized it until I met Rose."

Richard nodded. "I know she's ambitious and high maintenance, but I understand why."

"What do you mean?"

"You've seen her with her family. What did you think?"

Stephen took a bite of his sandwich and frowned. "She's daddy's little princess; she keeps pushing until she gets her way."

"Have you ever seen her with her entire family, I mean her parents and her brothers?"

"Yes, two years ago at Christmas."

Richard shifted his position. "Did she act differently?"

Stephen frowned. "Now that you mention it, she was uncharacteristically quiet. Her parents spoke to her brothers a lot but not to her. I thought it was because they weren't happy about me."

Richard studied his water bottle before answering. "I don't think so. I've talked to her several times, and I got the impression she pushes to get her own way to appear to be in control. She's daddy's princess; okay, what does a princess do? In medieval days, a princess was used to create a political alliance with a foreign country or a rival. I think she's received some pressure to marry someone her father approves of. Holding office is her way of demonstrating that she's more than a princess."

"I never thought of that." Stephen scratched his forehead.

"Hurry up and finish; we have to get moving, or we'll be late for the afternoon session."

Ashley answered her phone on the second ring. "Hello, Mother."

"Ashley, I know you're busy, so I won't keep you long. Can you come to the house for dinner tomorrow night?"

"Just a minute." Ashley stopped and checked the calendar on her phone. "Yes, I can make tomorrow. What time do you want me there?"

"Six thirty will be fine. Oh, and wear something nice. I'll see you tomorrow. Bye."

Ashley stared at her phone. "Great. Not again."

Chapter 17

The Announcement

John sat at the table in the conference room of the governor's office. The table was covered with topographical maps, books, and geological survey charts. His hand rested on a legal pad, and he stared at the ballpoint pen. What a wondrous invention. It was a far cry from the steel pens of his day. Of course, steel was better than quill, but this, you didn't even have to mix ink. It carried its own inkwell where the ink stayed fresh and ready to use. The ink dried quickly on the page and always looked smooth. It even came in different colors. He shook his head. Some of the things in this time were truly amazing.

"John?" Radnor stepped into the room. "How's the project coming?"

"Good. I'm almost finished." John leaned back in his chair and stretched.

"Have you seen Rachel?"

"No."

"I need her to get a message to the senators on the short list. Bartlett would like to meet with all of them during lunch." Radnor picked up one of the books and read the title.

"I can run the message for you." John smiled. This would be the perfect opportunity to have a quiet word with Ashley.

"No, I'd rather have Rachel do it. Her dad wants her to get to know the people in the legislature. She's been studying the photo book, but I want her to actually interact with the people and not just recognize the faces."

"I don't mind going with her and helping." John shifted in his chair.

"Naw, go ahead and get lunch if you like, but Rachel should do this by herself."

John nodded and turned back to his papers. As soon as he heard Radnor's footsteps disappear down the hall, he got up and headed for the senate.

He found Rachel standing by the entryway, just as he had the day before. "Hello, how are you today?"

Rachel turned to him. "Hey, John, it's good to see you. What are you doing here?"

John smiled. "Stretching my legs after doing hours of research for your father. Are you waiting for someone?"

"Yeah, Dad wants to meet with some of the senators during lunch, and Mason asked me to give them these notes." She held up a short stack of envelopes.

"Do you need some help? I can hand some of them out for you or point out who's who." If he could get hold of the stack, he'd pull out Ashley's and try to get a more private meeting with her later.

John had stepped forward to ask to see the stack when he glanced at the stairs and saw the governor's private secretary coming up. He clenched his hands into fists. Why wouldn't these stupid people leave him alone and let him do what he wanted? "Well, I'd best grab lunch while I can. I'll see you later." He turned and headed for the elevator.

Ashley glanced at the note in her hand and headed for the stairs. There wasn't much time to get to the governor's office and get back in time to have lunch before the session started again. When she reached the second floor, she found Richard waiting at the bottom of the stairs.

"Good, I was hoping to catch you before you went to lunch."

"I'm sorry, Richard; I've been called to the governor's office."

"That's okay. This will only take a second. I just wanted to tell you not to go to Stephen's announcement this afternoon."

Ashley bit her lip. "Actually, I wasn't planning to attend. Bartlett will have someone there watching the crowd, and it wouldn't help my bid for the lieutenant governor's slot if I show up supporting his opponent." She shifted on her feet.

"Exactly. Stephen asked me to speak to you. He didn't want you to feel guilty about missing the event. And he wishes you good luck in getting the appointment."

She looked surprised and then lowered her eyes. "Tell him thank you. You're going aren't you?"

"Of course."

"Good, you can tell me all about it over drinks tonight." She gave him a wink. "I'll come to the bar as soon as I'm done with my last meeting. Because none of Bartlett's people goes in there, it will be a safe place to meet. I really want to know all about the announcement. Now I have to get going, or I'll be late for Bartlett's meeting."

Richard grinned. "I'll see you tonight."

Ashley touched the doorknob to the governor's office and froze. Was he bringing all the candidates in to tell them his decision or only the losers? Her heart pounded, and her hand started to shake. She took a deep breath. This was not the time to show excitement or fear. And if he did choose someone else, well, she'd be standing in the front row at Stephen's announcement. She turned the knob and walked in.

Two of the other candidates on the short list were already there. She gave one a nod while Hampton came up to her.

"Ashley, you sit on the State Affairs Committee; do you think the chairman will allow a hearing on any bill to expel the federal government from Idaho lands?" He gave her that used-car-salesman smile again.

She kept her face blank. The man was obviously fishing for information. "I've not heard anything about a bill being put forth. I've heard rumors that it's being looked into by someone, but that's all."

She had a sinking feeling about her chances of getting the lieutenant governor's position. This slimy toad was exactly the sort of candidate Bartlett was looking for. Richard and Stephen were right. Bartlett wanted a yes-man, not a partner.

"Well, if something does get presented, let me know." He grinned at her.

And there's that creepy smile again. "Of course, Senator." She gave him her best smile.

The rest of the candidates arrived, followed by Bartlett and Radnor.

"Gentleman and lady," he gave a nod to Ashley. "I am still in the process of making my decision about the lieutenant governor's position. I called you all here to let you know that I will be contacting my choice on January twenty-fifth and making an announcement to the press that afternoon. I'm sorry this has taken so long, but as you all know, this is a very important decision. I will be speaking with each of you privately before making my final decision. Thank you for coming."

Radnor stepped forward. "Please don't mention any of this outside of this room. The press is harping at us daily for a decision, and we don't want those jackals to have any clue about what is going on until we are ready to announce."

With that, both he and the governor left the room. There was a general murmuring and several comments about the process, but Ashley didn't stay to hear them. She wanted to go somewhere and drown her disappointment, but there was still the afternoon session, so a drink was out of the question. She'd have to settle for lunch now and drinks later with Richard.

Stephen stood behind one of the pillars of the capital building. Rose stood beside him, wrapped in a heavy overcoat with a woolen scarf and hat. He smiled at her. She loved to wear hats, even though it wasn't really fashionable in this time. He was surprised when she told him that several of her clients were ordering hats with some of their clothing purchases. Maybe they'd make a comeback.

"Are you nervous?" Rose asked, looking up at him.

"No, more excited than nervous. I've been looking forward to this for a long time."

Stephen peered around the pillar. A large crowd was forming on the capitol steps. "Mandy has done a great job putting this together; she's even got Charlie and his mother down there handing out bumper stickers and yard signs." He stepped back and took Rose's hand. "I don't like leaving you here alone. Even for a few minutes. John is somewhere close; I'm sure of it."

Rose shuddered. "I'll be all right. Gabriel told you he'd protect me. I will trust in that."

Stephen leaned over and kissed her forehead. He glanced at his watch. It was almost time to start. He leaned around the pillar again and saw Mandy working her way through the crowd toward him. She stopped near the podium and said something to Senator Bellmore.

"Hey," Richard said beside him.

Stephen nearly jumped out of his skin. "Why are you sneaking up on me?"

"Well, I'd hardly call it sneaking. I'm stomping around in cowboy boots, for heaven's sake. You're just too preoccupied with your moment."

Stephen nodded. "Can you do me a favor and stand here with Rose until I call her to the podium. I don't want anyone to bother her, like a reporter or one of Bartlett's people."

"Sure, no problem. I feel honored that you trust me to protect your beautiful wife." Richard flashed Rose a grin, and she giggled.

"Hey, I said watch out for her, not flirt with her." Some of the tension left Stephen's shoulders.

"Listen, I'm helping you out; I'm entitled to some perks. Isn't that right, Rose?" Richard took her hand.

"Certainly, Richard. I feel quite safe under your protection."

Mandy, a plump, middle-aged woman with auburn hair, joined the group. She looked at Stephen. "Good, you're smiling. Now get ready to wow the crowd."

"I'm not sure about wowing them, but I'll talk to them." Stephen turned and gave Rose a quick kiss, and then he took a deep breath and stepped out from behind the pillar.

Senator Bellmore stood behind the podium. "Good afternoon, I am glad to see such a good turnout for today's announcement; it is my privilege to introduce Representative Stephen Winship. Many of you know him as the man who championed the Grocery Tax Relief Act last year. The bill passed both houses of the legislature but was unfortunately and rather dramatically vetoed by our current governor.

"I had the privilege of working with Stephen on that bill, and I have come to know him well. I am very proud to work with him on another more personal project, The Mentors Program. Representative Winship is the kind of man we need in the governor's office. He is genuinely concerned about the welfare of the people of this state, and that's something we truly need. With that, I am pleased to introduce Stephen Winship, the next governor of the State of Idaho."

There were shouts of support and applause as Stephen walked up to the microphone and shook hands with the old man.

"Thank you, Senator Bellmore for that kind introduction. As many of you know, the State of Idaho…"

Richard leaned toward Mandy. "How did you get Bellmore to do the introduction?"

Mandy grinned. "He volunteered. He plans to retire after this term, so he's not afraid of any reprisal from Bartlett. He genuinely likes Stephen and wants to see him replace the governor."

Richard nodded. "Well, he's a very good opener; he's well respected, and he's been in the senate for over twenty years. His opinion carries weight."

Mandy smiled. "I was delighted to get him. I couldn't think of anyone better."

Stephen was still speaking and obviously hitting his stride. "We need more high-paying jobs in the state. We have excellent higher education systems with the University of Idaho, Boise State University, and Idaho State University, but after our children graduate from these schools, they have to go out of state to find jobs." Stephen continued speaking of his plans to help draw business to Idaho and improve the necessary infrastructure to move the state forward economically. "Thank you all for coming out on this cold afternoon, and I welcome your support in the coming campaign. Now I'd like to introduce my beautiful wife, Rose."

Rose walked over to the podium. People applauded.

"Idaho is a great state, and it can have a very good future if we all work together. Thank you again for coming out, and God bless the great state of Idaho."

Lots of applause and shouts came from those assembled. The television cameras scanned the crowd to show the turnout on the six o'clock news.

Mandy turned to Richard. "I'd better get down there. The press will start questioning him, and I should be there. Good to see you, Richard. Thanks for coming."

"Oh, I wouldn't have missed it."

At the far edges of the crowd, John stood, staring at the podium. This should have been his life. He should have stood outside the building that housed the territorial legislature. Rose should have been standing at his side, not at this stranger's. John clenched his fists. They'd pay. He'd make them pay. Rose didn't get to have the perfect life, not after robbing him of his. He growled, and a woman standing nearby glanced at him uneasily. Why couldn't he connect with Ashley? He walked away from the crowd and headed for the sidewalk, intending to enter the capitol from a side door.

Radnor came up to him. "John, I'm surprised to see you out here. Are you looking for another job?"

John stared at him in puzzlement. "What?"

Radnor gave him an odd look. "You do realize that you work for the sitting governor, and you're at a rally held by his opponent?"

"Oh, I was taking a walk outside to stretch my legs and saw this event happening. I just stopped to listen to what the speaker was saying. He has a very pretty wife."

Radnor glanced up at the stage. "Yes, he does. Excuse me, I see someone I need to talk to." He walked straight over to one of the camera operators from a local TV station.

John flared his nostrils. He scanned the crowd for Ashley, but there were too many people bundled up against the weather to be able to tell if she were here. He looked back at Rose standing next to her new husband, infuriated by the look of love and pride on her face. He scowled.

In the time she had been his wife, he'd never seen her look at him that way. He wanted to run up to the podium and pull her away from that man. No one took away something that was his.

Not in his wildest dreams did he ever think he'd be brought down to this state of affairs. Dreams. He wanted to smack himself in the head. Of course, that was the answer. If he couldn't get to Ashley during the day, then he would do it at night. This posed a problem. It took energy to invade someone's dreams, and Abaddon wouldn't give him any more. That meant he had to spend less time visible during the day to save up enough to use at night. It would take a day or two, but he'd find a way.

He took one more glance at Rose and her husband. Soon he'd have his revenge.

Chapter 18
Surprises

Ashley walked into Richard's bar and stopped. The place was absolutely packed. Several televisions played basketball games, two had music videos, and one showed *Gone with the Wind*. Rock music played in the background, and from everywhere came the sounds of people laughing, shouting at the games, or having conversations. The entire place buzzed with an air of excitement. No wonder Richard spent so much time in this place. The atmosphere was intoxicating and addictive.

She made her way through the crowd, glancing at each of the tables, hoping to spot him in this mass of people. A waitress carrying a tray full of drinks stopped.

"Senator Halliday, he's waiting for you. Let me deliver these drinks, and I'll take you to him." She disappeared into the throng before Ashley could answer.

In a surprisingly short time, the waitress returned. "Follow me." She led the way through the maze of tables to the far edge of the large bar that dominated one wall of the room. Richard sat at a small table in the corner nursing a drink. He looked up as Ashley approached and broke out in a smile.

The waitress nodded at Richard and headed in another direction.

Richard tapped the stool next to him, and Ashley slid onto it.

"Is it always this noisy at night?" Ashley set her purse down and unbuttoned her coat.

"Here, let me help you with that." Richard got up, stepped behind her, and removed her coat. He folded it over the empty chair at their table. He sat back on his stool and waved at the bartender. "It's usually busy at night, but this evening is setting a record. I couldn't even sit in my usual place at the bar." He pointed to it. Every chair along the bar was full of people staring at the game playing on the two televisions mounted on the wall. "What would you like to drink?"

"I'd like a margarita."

"Are you hungry? I can order us up some snacks or something more solid?" Richard took a sip of his drink.

Ashley stretched on her chair. "Something to eat would be great. Order what ever you want; I'll find something to nibble on."

The bartender came over, and Richard gave him instructions.

A loud shout went up in one section of the bar. Ashley turned toward the commotion. "What's going on tonight?"

"Lots and lots of basketball, there are a couple of college games and one NBA game. Notice how people have formed into groups around the various television sets. You can tell who they're rooting for." Richard took another sip of his drink.

"Okay, so why the music videos and the movie?"

Richard shrugged his shoulders. "Not everyone likes basketball, so I try to have something else for those customers to watch."

The bartender returned with Ashley's drink and large plate of nachos followed by a waitress carrying smaller plates and flatware. When they left, Richard leaned over, took her hand, and squeezed it. "Thanks for coming."

She smiled. "It's my pleasure; I wanted your company this evening. How was Stephen's announcement?" She removed her hand from his grasp, picked up her glass, and took a sip. "Wow, this is strong. You may need to call me a cab."

He laughed. "No need. I have a car service that picks me up each night and takes me home. I don't want to add my name to that honor roll of legislators with DUI arrests." He took another sip.

"Richard, you really surprise me. You think of all the little details don't you? Oh, these nachos are good."

Another yell from the crowd interrupted his answers. Richard looked over his shoulder. "Gonzaga must have scored again. I don't think of all the details, but I try to think of the most logical ones. I learned the hard way that the old adage is true; the devil really is in the details." He shifted on his stool. "Stephen's announcement went very well. Mandy really is a first-rate political consultant. She had the capitol steps filled with supporters all standing in the cold to cheer for their candidate. The press cameras recorded everything, and he made the six o'clock news. Bartlett is probably at home sticking pins in a little Stephen doll."

She laughed. "I hope Stephen wins. I really want to see Bartlett defeated."

Richard raised an eyebrow. "Aren't you trying to be his right-hand man as lieutenant governor?"

Ashley frowned. "I was until I realized today that you and Stephen were right. He will only nominate a yes-man to that post."

Richard reached for her hand again. "What happened, Ashley?"

"Bartlett had a meeting with the members of the short list. He's making his announcement on the twenty-fifth." She took a deep breath. "I sat there looking at all the people in the room, and I realized I was only there for show. He was probably hoping the possibility of power would go to my head, and I'd betray you and Stephen." She shifted on her stool. "It was so tempting. I want to be governor. I want to prove that I can do the job." She looked at his face and didn't see disgust or pity.

He squeezed her hand. "Ashley, I have complete confidence that you will one day be the governor of this state; it just won't be now."

"Thanks, Richard. I appreciate your support." She gave him a smile.

"Hey, no need to thank me. I really believe you will do it. All you need to do is to gain experience, name recognition in the senate, and then, after a few terms, make a run. I'm not just saying this to make you feel better. I have faith in you. You're smart and politically savvy. Plan your path to your goal, and don't look for shortcuts. Be patient and work hard; you'll get there. Good grief, I sound like a fortune cookie." He leaned over and kissed her.

They broke apart, and Ashley ran a hand along his face. "Richard, there is something happening between us, and we both know it. I...I want to take this slowly. I want to do this right. I thought I had something before, but I was wrong. Stephen is a good man, but he wasn't the right man. I want to make sure I have the right man this time."

Richard smiled. "Don't worry; we can take this as slowly as we need to. There is no reason to hurry." He took a sip of whiskey. "We're still on for dinner and a show after Bartlett makes his choice for lieutenant governor?

She laughed. "*'The Phantom of the Opera'* is starting next week. I want you to get tickets for the Friday after the announcement."

"Your wish is my command."

Gabriel watched the two at the bar and smiled. All the pieces were falling into place; it was time to make the next major move on the board.

For the next few days, John didn't even attempt to see Ashley. He stuck to his assignment and tried to use as little energy as possible. He even disappeared several times in the day to preserve the power Abaddon gave him. Finally, he felt he had enough to make an attempt. Now all he had to do was wait for a time when Abaddon was occupied with something else, so he could slip away. The opportunity finally arrived the following Friday.

Abaddon laughed at John's feeble attempts to deceive him. Still, the fool seemed determined to continue with his plan. Perhaps a greater infusion of power would help move things along. There was, after all, only a small window of opportunity in which to hinder Gabriel's plans before the angel figured out what was happening and took steps to stop it. It would be best to inflict as much damage as possible before that happened.

Ashley walked into her apartment and nearly collapsed on the sofa. Her ears hurt almost as much as her feet after being stopped and courted by more lobbyists then there were ants at a picnic. Bartlett was doing a full court press to get the federal Enhanced Education Plan implemented in the state. Apparently, there were two lobbying firms working the issue in the legislature. Richard was right; Bartlett did want to get his hands on that federal money.

Ashley slipped off her boots and stretched out. If the rest of the legislative sessions were like today, she'd never survive it. Closing her eyes and rubbing her temples, she started to relax; lying down felt so good. After a while, she shifted her position. If she didn't get up soon, she'd fall asleep with all her clothes on. Groaning, she sat up; it was time to get ready for bed.

Once her head hit the pillow, she rolled on her side expecting to fall asleep quickly, but her mind began flashing a recap of the day's events. It took almost an hour for her to fall asleep.

John had to be careful. His energy was limited, and he needed to make the most of it. Having walked in Ashley's dreams before, he had to make sure she was asleep before making the transition. The best way was to make his attempt around three thirty in the morning. Abaddon would not bother him until seven, so he had a few hours.

He stood in the mirror, watching her sleep. She was restless tonight. Best begin this quickly before she woke herself up. John stepped through the mirror, walked over to the bed, and sat down on the edge. Even in sleep with her hair spread out over the pillow, she looked so beautiful. He closed his eyes and concentrated.

John wandered through Ashley's dream. She was sitting at her desk in the senate arguing with another senator. This scene wouldn't work for what he wanted to do, so he slowly changed the background and moved her mind to the place he had prepared.

Ashley watched the senate chamber fade away and slowly change into a row of cottonwood trees. A cool breeze blew through the leaves and the sound of running water came from behind them. She remembered this place as she made her way to the river. It was much cooler under the branches, and she shivered. The sight of the fast-moving water tumbling over rocks relaxed the tension in her shoulders. A path ran along the bank, weaving among the trees and bushes. She followed it for a short way. A rustling through the leaves on her right made her stop. A man stepped out from behind a tree and walked toward her.

Her heart pounded until she saw his face,

"John, what are you doing here?"

131

"Hello, how delightful to see you." He came up and stood in front of her. "I got bored with my political work and wanted to stretch my legs. I didn't expect to see anyone out here." He waved a hand at their surroundings. "It's a beautiful day to take a walk along the river. Would you like to join me?"

Ashley nodded and took his offered arm. "I love the spring when all the trees and plants along the river start blooming. It feels like the whole world is beginning again."

They strolled along the river making light and friendly conversation. The wind picked up, and Ashley started to shiver.

"Come, my house isn't far away. I'll have the servants make some hot coffee or tea. It's this way.

The scene blurred, and Ashley found herself standing in a wide entryway. A young woman came in from one of the side doors.

"Molly, make us up a tray of coffee and tea. If cook has any treats, like tarts or cake, bring them along." He turned to Ashley. "Come into the parlor. There will be a nice fire, and you'll be able to get warm." He opened the door and motioned for her to enter.

Ashley walked into a well-furnished room. The walls were made of a rich dark paneling that matched the wood of the tables and the chairs. Candelabra hung on several walls, and all the candles were lighted. Portraits also hung on the walls, and small tables stood next to each of the large wingback chairs. She walked over to one near the fireplace and sat down. John sat in the chair beside her.

Molly entered the room bearing a tray and set it on the table next to John. She gave a quick bow and left the room.

"Would you like coffee or tea?"

"Oh, coffee please." She rubbed her hands together and held them out to the fire. "This is a very lovely house. Where is the rest of your family?"

"My father is inspecting one of his properties, and my mother is visiting friends." He poured coffee into a fine china cup and placed it on Ashley's table. "Would you like milk or sugar? We also have tea cakes."

"Just milk and sugar, please."

He set a sugar bowl and small milk pitcher beside her. "What does your father do?" she asked while spooning sugar.

"My family is in the mining business."

"Is that what you do for Bartlett, consult with him on the state's natural resources?"

"Yes, that and other special projects, but enough shoptalk. I want to know about you. What is a beautiful woman like you doing in politics?"

Ashley laughed. "I like politics. I have been fascinated by the process for a long time. I enjoy being in the heart of what makes things happen for the people of this state."

"Don't you get bored with parliamentary procedure and all the lobbying for your vote?" John picked up a teacake and took a bite.

"The lobbyists are very tiring, but the procedure and the steps it takes to get a bill introduced and passed, that I find interesting." She took a sip of her coffee and hung on to the cup to help warm her fingers.

"Are you sure you don't want a teacake? Cook is very talented, and her treats are delicious."

"No, thank you. I have a dinner appointment this evening; a dessert now would be too much."

John shifted in his chair. "Really, a dinner appointment, business or pleasure?"

Ashley laughed. "That's an interesting question. I'm having dinner at my parents' house. They have invited one of my father's clients and his son to join us."

She took another sip of coffee to avoid speaking further. It was a pleasure to see her parents, but her father meant this as a business dinner, the business of marrying off his daughter.

John stood up and paced in front of the fireplace. "Your father sounds like mine, always using a family gathering as an excuse to create a business opportunity or further one of his plans. Have you ever been married, Ashley?"

The question caught her by surprise, and her spoon rattled against her cup. "I was engaged once but never married. Have you?"

"Yes, for only a year. She contracted pneumonia and died."

"I'm sorry, John. You must have been devastated."

Their conversation was interrupted by the return of the maid. "Will you be needin' anything else, sir?"

"No, Molly," he said rather harshly.

Ashley caught his eye, and he turned back to the maid and spoke kindly. "Thank you, Molly, that will be all."

The maid gave a quick bow and left the room. John walked over to the door, and Ashley heard the click of the lock.

She hastily set her cup on its saucer, spilling a bit of coffee over the sides. "Thank you for your hospitality, John. I really must be going now. I have several things I need to do this afternoon before I head to my parents' house."

Before she could stand, his hand rested on her shoulder. "You really don't have to leave yet."

His hand moved up and stroked her cheek.

Ashley sat bolt upright, panting. It took a moment for her mind to register her surroundings. She sat up in bed, in her bedroom and alone. She clutched her chest and got her breathing under control.

A dream, that's all it was. A crazy and very-detailed dream. Except for that feeling of evil stroking her skin.

John flew through the mirror and landed hard against his headstone. His fingers tingled, and his arm ached as if he'd been smacked by a heavy tree branch. He moved his hand, trying to get the stiffness out of the muscles. Ashley had some sort of "protection" placed on her. He didn't feel anything when he touched her shoulder, but her face.... He held up his hand and saw burn marks on his fingers and every place that had touched her skin. Damn. Now what? He couldn't let Abaddon find out what happened. He licked a finger to stop the burning feeling. Hopefully, this would be gone by morning.

Chapter 19
Problems

Bartlett paced his office like a very large bear in a very small cage. "The audacity, the arrogance, the stupidity…" He swung his arm and knocked a stack of books off his desk. "How dare that little pip-squeak challenge me."

A knock on the door stopped him in his tracks. "What?"

Mason came in and closed the door behind him. "Sir, you really need to keep your voice down."

"Don't come in my office and tell me how to behave. Dammit Mason, I thought you were going to deal with this pest last year. Now he's running against me." He started pacing again.

"This shouldn't be a surprise to you. When he managed to get his tax bill through the house and senate, it was only a matter of time before he announced. I don't know what you're so upset about. You can beat him." Mason pulled out one of the office chairs and sat down.

"I spoke to our campaign manager, and we have a fundraiser scheduled in two weeks. We are working on our first mailing listing all the things you have done for this state. It will go out in the last week of February. I've got people cleaning out the campaign office, and we'll have it up and running by the end of next week. Things will be fine."

Bartlett leaned against the desk, panting. "I didn't want to have to run against him, that's all. I can't stand the bloody Boy Scout. He's going to pick at everything I do, and I'm going to have to play defense. We already know he's squeaky clean, and trying to start rumors about him and tarnish his character didn't work. Mark my words; this is going to be the toughest campaign I have ever had." He winced and reached into his pocket, pulling out a small bottle.

"What's that?"

"Huh? Oh, this? It's nothing. Something the doctor gave me for when I get upset. Don't worry about it. Worry about how we are going to win this election."

"Russ, are you sure you're all right? You look a bit pale and sweaty."

"I'm okay; I just need to sit down. Get me a glass of water." Bartlett moved around the desk and sat heavily on his chair. He opened the bottle and took out a pill. He stuck it under his tongue and quickly hid the bottle before Mason could see what it contained.

Mason came back with a cold bottle of water. He took the top off before handing it to Bartlett. "I wanted to talk about the possibility of a land bill this session. I have feelers out in the house and senate, but there is no mention of a bill yet in any of the committees. Someone is having Theorem Data Technologies research federal lands. The state's files on fire suppression were requested, and I have a friend in D.C. who told me that a lot of the Forest Service's files were requested as well. Someone is dead serious about this."

Bartlett drained half the bottle before he answered. "Is there any way to get information out of the company about who requested the information?"

"No, that is part of their appeal. Their client list is strictly confidential. I can tell you, though, that Paul Miller has been seen with Marion Austin and Frank Woodward."

Bartlett slammed the bottle on the desk. "Dammit, I'd bet good money it's going to come from that group. I'm sure Winship and Fowler are up to their necks in it. Get some of our people working on a possible way to block a hypothetical land bill. Even if it isn't Winship, I want to have a way to stop any bill dealing with federal land within the state's borders. The last thing I want is to get into a pissing match with the feds. I'm going to have to raise a lot of out-of-state money for this campaign, and a bill like that could jeopardize my ability to raise it. And if my daughter is in yet, I want to see her. Now, I have some work to do."

"Sure. Russ, I'll see to it."

"Are you still on for presenting next Friday?" Stephen spoke quietly into his desk phone. Around him, the members of the house were listening to Representative Pelt debate the merits of a memorial for members of the Idaho National Guard.

Richard's voice came over the line. "I'm getting a report from Sam and Paul at the bar around five. Do you want to meet with us and go over the findings?"

"Let me check with Rose and see how long she'll be at the shop tonight. I'll let you know."

The Speaker announced that the house would be voting on this measure. Stephen hung up the phone.

The voting lasted a few minutes, after which the Speaker asked for a motion to adjourn.

Stephen picked up his phone and called Rose. Clair answered on the first ring.

"I didn't expect you to pick up so fast. Is everything all right?"

"Oh, everything is fine. I had just hung up with a client when you called. Rose is doing a fitting right now. Do you want me to interrupt her?"

"No, I just called to find out how long she'll be working tonight."

"We have two more fittings after this one. I'd say we'd be done around seven. I already called the car and told them to be here at that time."

"Great, thank you, Clair. I'm going to a meeting with Richard and a few others. Tell Rose I'll see her at home."

"Sure thing, Stephen."

"Thanks, Clair."

Stephen picked up his briefcase and packed up his papers.

Richard looked up when Stephen reached his desk. "Well?"

"Lead on; I have until seven."

Richard's cell phone rang, and he pulled it out of his pocket. "Can I meet you in a minute? It's my sister, so I have to take this call."

"Sure, I'll drive over to the bar now. I want my car close when I leave tonight. I'll see you over there." Stephen left the house chamber.

Richard answered the phone. "Hey, sis, how much do you need?" Richard leaned back in his chair.

"Richard, I don't always call about money."

"Okay then. Lizzy, how is your husband?" The last few representatives left the house chamber, and Richard was alone.

"Chip is fine."

He snorted. "Well it's good to know the liquor is holding out."

"Richard, Chip works hard each day, and he's in better shape than you are."

He rolled his eyes. Clarence Buford Tanner, also known as Chip, worked as golf pro at one of the private clubs in Phoenix.

"And how is your son, Jimmy?"

"Your nephew is fine. Stop being such a jerk."

"All right, I'll go back to my original question. How much do you need?"

"Look, the cruise at Christmas was a lot more expensive than I expected it to be. I want to call a trust meeting and get a distribution. Okay?"

Richard heard a few muffled swear words. "Why didn't you just say that in the first place? When do you want to hold the meeting?"

"Chip and I will fly in the morning of the twenty-eighth. If we could hold the meeting around noon and get the check issued that afternoon, we'll fly back on Friday morning."

"Liz, the legislature is in session now. I can't take off in the middle of the day."

"Richard, I need the money, and I expect you to make time for a board meeting."

"All right, how about you catch a later flight, and I'll have a car pick you up at the airport? Mrs. Holcomb can cook a special dinner at the house, and we'll hold the meeting in the evening. I can have the accountant messenger over the check in the morning before you have to leave to catch a flight home."

He could hear grumbling on the line as his sister explained his proposal to someone, probably her deadbeat husband.

"Okay, that will work. We'll see you on the twenty-eighth. Goodbye, big brother."

"Bye, Liz."

Great, now he had to deal with his sister and her drunkard of a husband the night before his bill went to the committee chair.

Richard walked over to the bar and found Stephen already seated with the Miller brothers at the usual reserved table in the back corner.

"Hello, gentlemen, sorry I'm late." He glanced around the table. "Hasn't anybody offered you any food or drinks?"

Stephen laughed. "They tried repeatedly, but we told them we'd wait until you got here."

"Well then, let's get this meeting started." He signaled one of the waitresses. The woman arrived at the table and handed out menus.

"What can I bring you to drink?" she asked, pulling out a notepad.

When each man had ordered, Richard turned to her. "Angie, I'll have the usual. Bring us some mini pizzas, nachos, and chicken wings. Thanks, Angie."

He waited until she was out of earshot. "Okay, what have you found out?"

Sam cleared his throat. "Well, I must say when you first brought me this project, I expected to find waste and poor management by the federal government, but I had no idea how bad it actually was." He reached into his briefcase and pulled out a stack of files. He placed one folder after another on the table, giving a brief description of his findings on all the subjects requested. By the time he set the last folder on the table, Richard and Stephen were sitting with their mouths open.

Richard shook his head. "Wow, that exceeds even my low expectations. This is exactly what I was looking for. What do you think, Stephen?"

Stephen nodded. "There is more than enough here to make a compelling case." He turned to the other men. "Is this the final format of the data, or will you put it into charts and graphs?"

The waitress returned with their drinks, temporarily putting a halt to the conversation. After she left, Sam took a sip of his drink and then addressed Richard.

"We can present this data any way you want. Do you have anything specific in mind?"

Richard leaned back in his chair. "My plan is to beat them over the head with the facts. I want each incident of fire listed, along with a list of the property damage, the timber loss due to insect damage, the works. I want it shown in charts and graphs, and in spreadsheets with dollar amounts. Can you do all that by January twenty-ninth, so I can go prepare over the weekend and present it on Monday, February first?"

The two Millers looked at each other and both nodded. Paul answered. "Yeah, we can have it ready by then."

Chapter 20
Dinner

Ashley pulled up in her parent's driveway and wanted to turn around again. Why did her father do this? This had to be the fifth time he'd set up a dinner and invited some colleague or local businessman along with his bachelor son. She felt like she was on display, a sort of mannequin in a window wearing a dress and inviting someone to buy it.

Her mother moved the drapes and glanced out the window. Drat, she'd been spotted. No chance of slipping away and calling in some excuse to miss the dinner. Might as well make the best of it.

She turned off the engine and checked her lipstick in the rearview mirror. She closed her eyes and found her composure. If she smiled and remained polite but uninterested, maybe everyone would get the hint that she didn't want to be auctioned off to the highest bidder.

Her mother started in the moment she walked through the door and took off her coat. "Ashley, couldn't you have worn something a bit nicer? You know that your father has invited company this evening."

Ashley stretched her fingers and then tightened them into a fist. She was wearing an expensive and well-designed business suit in royal blue, with a skirt with a matching jacket, a white silk blouse, and a red silk scarf. "Mother, I came here directly from the capitol. I didn't have time to change. Besides, this is a nice suit, and it's not like I showed up in jeans and a T-shirt."

Her mother frowned. "Very well dear, come and help me in the kitchen. Our guests will be here any minute."

Ashley reluctantly followed her mother.

The smell of roasting beef filled the room. She noticed the best china was set out on the counter awaiting the food. Whomever her dad had invited, he definitely wanted to impress them.

"Ashley, I picked up rolls at the bakery today. Can you put them in the bread basket, the one under the hutch?"

"So who has Dad invited this evening?" Ashley opened the bakery bag, and the smell of fresh croissants and sourdough rolls filled the air.

"He's invited Dr. Floyd Henderson and his son, Brandon. His son has finished dentistry school and will be joining his dad's practice." Her mother removed green beans from the burner and poured them into the strainer in the sink.

"Are we serving dinner right away? Dad usually likes to have drinks first."

"Not this time. Floyd has some sort of surgery he has to perform in the morning, so there won't be any alcoholic drinks."

Ashley hid her smile. Her mother was tactfully ignoring the fact that the Hendersons were Mormons. They wouldn't be drinking, whether they had a surgery in the morning or not. "So, what do you know about Brandon?"

Her mother put the green beans in a china serving bowl and sprinkled pine nuts over them. "Well, he is very athletic. He went to college on some type of sports scholarship. He did well at dental school. Floyd says his son is ready to settle down and start a family."

Ashley nearly dropped the roll she was holding. Is that what her father thought of her? She was some type of broodmare, and he was simply trying to find the best stallion to bring into the family.

She cleared her throat. "Then we should have a pleasant dinner because I am not ready to either settle down or start a family."

Her father picked that moment to come into the kitchen. He glanced between them. "What were you two discussing?"

"Nothing much, Father. I was just asking Mother what she knew about our dinner guests." Ashley finished filling the basket and turned toward the dining room.

"Ashley, let's keep the political talk to a minimum. I don't want to put our guests to sleep in the middle of their dinner. Norma, this smells fantastic." He leaned over and gave his wife a kiss on the forehead.

The doorbell rang, and he strode out of the kitchen to let his guests in.

Ashley wasn't sure what to expect, but when Brandon walked in the door, her jaw dropped. Brandon stood well over six feet. He had a handsome face and thick, sandy-blond hair. His deep-blue eyes landed on her, and he gave her a warm smile.

Her father motioned to Ashley to step forward. "Floyd, this is my daughter Ashley. Ashley, Dr. Floyd Henderson, and his son, Dr. Brandon Henderson.

It didn't escape her notice that her father had included the titles of both men, but left off her own title of state senator. That hurt. She thought he was proud of her winning her senate seat. He had given Stephen enough grief during the election when Bartlett was causing trouble, and it looked like the trouble might spill over onto her race. Now her father seemed to be treating her victory like a one-time thing, a trophy for a speech or project but achieved and left behind in favor of the next accomplishment. She couldn't remember her father treating Bill's or Tom's successes in the same way.

Ashley held out her hand. "I'm pleased to meet you both."

Brandon's hand felt very warm to the touch, and she wondered if he'd worn heated gloves on the drive over.

"Come and sit down, gentlemen. I believe dinner is ready."

Her father escorted the men into the dining room while Ashley helped her mother bring in the food. She brought in the last dish and went in to take her seat, only to find her chair had been moved to the other side of the table, putting her next to Brandon. She controlled the urge to roll her eyes. *Could her parents be any more obvious?*

Her father asked Floyd if he wanted to say grace, and the man nodded and began to pray aloud. When he'd finished, everyone picked up a serving bowl and started filling their plates.

Ashley took only a spoonful of each item. Her mother was a very good cook. After she'd given up her career as an accountant to be a housewife and mother, she'd taken every cooking class she could find, including classes on the internet.

Growing up, family meals ranged from rich and exotic cuisines to strange and scary experiments. Her mother had hammered into her the need to keep her portions small and her weight under control.

As a child she had hated that, watching her brothers and father pile their plates with all the tasty goodies while she and her mother had only a spoonful or two of each item. By the time she'd reached junior high school, her mother's wisdom became apparent and the strategy had become a habit.

Her father's voice interrupted her thoughts. "So, Brandon, are you glad to be back home after all your schooling?"

"Yes, sir, it's been a long ten years, but I'm ready to start work." He put a forkful of scalloped potatoes in his mouth.

Her mom set down her glass of sparkling cider. "I thought dental school only took four years."

"Yes, ma'am, it normally does. I took an extra two years to study a specialty. We plan to add endodontics to our practice." He scooped up another forkful of potatoes. "This is delicious, Mrs. Halliday."

"What is endodontics?" her mom asked.

Brandon opened his mouth to answer, but his father beat him to it. "It's dealing with root canal therapy, trying to save a broken or diseased tooth. I have run into a lot of these problems during my years of practice and have had to refer my patients to a specialist to deal with them. Now Brandon has the ability to do the work, and we can take care of our patients better in-house than sending them elsewhere." He picked up his knife and started cutting into his prime rib.

"That is a very wise business decision, Floyd. The more you can offer your patients in a familiar and friendly atmosphere, the more patients you are likely to have." Her dad started in on his own prime rib.

The conversation lagged for a few minutes while everyone concentrated on their food, and then Floyd spoke again. "What do you do, Ashley?"

Before she could answer, her father stepped in. "Ashley has her own interior design company." He turned to her. "Didn't you just finish redecorating the offices of a pediatric practice?"

This was really too much; it was time to take back control and show her dad she wasn't going to put up with this little princess routine any more. "Yes, Dad, I did that over the Christmas holidays. I only have two projects I'm working on now because the legislature is in session, and I serve as a state senator."

That brought the conversation to a halt. Floyd gaped at her, and Brandon frowned.

"You work in politics?" he asked.

She wanted to laugh, but she knew that would really upset her parents. The way everyone was reacting, you'd think she had just announced that she moonlighted as a stripper.

"I've worked in politics for years, but I finally ran for office in the last election and won my senate seat. Do you have any interest in politics, Brandon?"

"Well, no not really. It always struck me as rather controlling, all these politicians making rules and trying to run other people's lives."

"Unfortunately, there are a lot of people in politics like that, but there are also those who are trying to make things better. Last year, I helped with the effort to get the sales tax removed from food. We got it through both sides of the legislature before Governor Bartlett had his little dramatic fit and vetoed it on the senate floor."

"Ashley, we really don't need to discuss politics at the table." Her father gave her a firm glance.

"That's all right, Everett, I don't mind. I was very much in favor of that bill. It is ridiculous to charge people on the food that they eat. We are taxed enough on other things; they don't need to tax food as well. The food tax really affects low-income people." Floyd looked genuinely interested in the discussion. He gave Ashley an approving smile.

Brandon still looked puzzled. "How can you run a business and be a legislator?"

"Well, the legislature is only in session about three months out of the year. We start the second week of January, and we are

145

usually out by April. Sometimes it runs a little longer, but that is rare. The early part of the session is slow, but it builds up, and toward the end, we are putting in a lot of hours. My interior design business isn't really affected much by the three-month break. People are usually getting their taxes figured out anyway, and I've found they don't make design decisions during that time. The two careers work very well together." She put a little more emphasis on the word "career."

She glanced over at her mother and saw her smile as she buttered a roll. Good, at least Mom understood. She loved her mom and respected her choice, but it was her mother's choice, not hers. She couldn't really say what the future held, but she wouldn't be a stay-at-home housewife, and she needed a man who understood that. She picked up her glass of cider and smiled. Richard understood that. Look at how he encouraged her to plan out her run for the governor's office.

The conversation around the table moved on to the topic of sports; Ashley made a few comments here and there, but her mission was accomplished. She glanced over at Brandon and watched him discussing basketball with her father. Brandon was a very handsome and well-built man, but a good husband was more than eye candy. Watching Stephen and Rose together had taught her that. This time she wanted a real soul mate. Someone who understood her and would support the things she wanted to do in life. Someone she could respect and help, a real partner. She flashed back to Richard and their meeting at the bar. *I wonder what he's doing tomorrow for breakfast.*

Ashley looked *up from the table* in time to see the waiter guiding Richard over to her. "Good morning. I'm so glad you could join me for breakfast."

"I'm delighted you called. I wanted to see you this weekend, but this morning was the only time I had free, so your timing was perfect." Richard reached over the table and gave her hand a squeeze.

Ashley laughed. "Yes, I never realized how hectic things would get during the legislative session. I only have two interior design jobs to do, but my only time to work on them is the weekends."

"I know. I have three different sports parties at the bar this weekend. The weather is lousy, and people are bored. Unless they ski, most of them are having a serious case of cabin fever, so they make any excuse to get out of the house." He picked up the menu. "I haven't eaten at the Country Club in a long time. I have a membership, but I use it only for golf in the summer."

Ashley gestured around the room. "I like to bring my clients here when we have a lot of decisions to make. The food is good, and the atrium-like atmosphere is always relaxing."

The dining room at the Country Club was built in the shape of a half circle and had large glass windows. Planters built along the lower edges of the window glass contained vines and blooming plants. Most of the vines grew along the window supports and up to the ceiling like ivy on the outside of an old building. They gave the room a spring atmosphere, even in the dead of winter.

A waiter came up to their table. "Good morning." He handed them each a cloth napkin with their flatware rolled inside. "Can I bring you each one of our signature mimosas?"

Ashley smiled. "I'd love one. Richard?"

"I'd like a Bloody Mary."

"I'll bring them while you decide on your order." The waiter left the table.

A moment later, a teenage boy came up with a small coffee cart. He placed a carafe of coffee on the table along with cups, cream, and sugar. He also set down a small pitcher of ice water and two glasses with ice.

Richard poured them each a glass of water and a cup of coffee. "So, what sounds good for breakfast?"

"I'm having their brandy and berries crepes." Ashley added sugar and cream to her coffee and was suddenly reminded of having coffee in John's house. She shivered as she thought of that horrible dream

"A mimosa and brandied berries for breakfast? Miss Halliday, do we need to discuss a drinking problem?"

Ashley laughed. "Look who's talking, Mr. Whiskey day and night."

The waiter returned with their drinks. "Have you decided?"

Ashley gave him her order. Richard ordered eggs Benedict. When the waiter left, Richard sipped his drink and settled more comfortably in his chair. "So, how was dinner at your folks?"

"The good news is I think they will finally stop trying to match me up. The bad news is my father will probably try to tear apart anyone I bring home."

Richard grinned. "I'm up for the challenge."

Ashley reached across the table and squeezed his hand. "How did the meeting go with the Millers?"

"Great." Richard explained everything the data showed and how it would help his bill. He didn't stop speaking until the waiter arrived with their breakfast.

They ate together in companionable silence for a while. Richard set down his fork. "I have a favor to ask of you."

"Really, what do you need?"

"Well, my sister and her husband are coming into town on Thursday. We will be having dinner at my house, and I would like you to come and meet them." He picked up his coffee.

"I'd love to meet your sister. What time do you want me there?"

"Six o'clock, but that's not the only reason I'm asking you to come. I also need you to protect me from her." He took a sip.

"What? Protect you? What do you mean?"

"Well, she and I are nothing alike. I guess the best way to describe her is New Age. She's into tarot cards, herbal remedies, and all things supernatural, and she tries to convert the world to her beliefs. I need you as a buffer between us, as well as wanting to introduce you." He looked down at the tablecloth, and his ears turned pink.

"Richard Fowler, are you embarrassed by your sister?"

"Not to put too fine a point on it, yes. She's a complete fruit loop."

"What's her husband like?"

"I don't know. I've never seen him sober."

Ashley laughed. "This sounds more entertaining than tickets to the theater. I will definitely come. It will be interesting to meet her and see another side of you." She glanced at her watch. "I'd better hurry up. I have to meet my client in half an hour."

Chapter 21
The Lieutenant Governor

Ashley shivered on the capitol steps. People stood bunched in groups for warmth while waiting for the governor to come out and make his announcement. Camera crews kept their machines covered with plastic against the light snow. Two of the news reporters stomped their feet, trying to stay warm. Obviously Bartlett hadn't taken the weather into consideration when he picked this date to announce the new lieutenant governor. At least Stephen had better weather for his announcement.

Only the senate and a few citizens were out in the cold to witness the event. Her committee chair had let them out early so they could attend; after all, the new person would be pro tem of the senate and preside over their sessions. She expected the house members to be out any minute now and kept checking for them.

When no messenger had pulled her out of her two committee meetings that morning, she knew for certain Bartlett had picked someone else. It stung a bit, but the relief of not having to deal with Bartlett every day made her feel better about everything. At least now she didn't have to hide the fact that she was seeing Richard.

One of the side doors opened, and members of the house stepped outside to join the rest of the crowd. Everyone was so bundled up against the weather; she wasn't sure if she would recognize Richard when he came out.

She pulled a bright red scarf out of her pocket and wrapped it around her neck. She had sent him a text earlier to be on the look out for it. It seemed a more dignified way for him to locate her than for her to stand there waving her hands.

It worked. She saw him exit the building with Stephen and point to her. A few minutes later, he stood beside her along with Stephen, Marion, Paul, and Frank.

Richard leaned close to her. "We have a small bet going. I think Bartlett will pick Hampton and so does Stephen, but Marion and Frank think it will be Senator Mitch Simpson. Paul is undecided. Who do you think it will be?"

She laughed. "Well, since he can't name himself as lieutenant governor, I agree with you; it will be Hampton. What's the bet?"

"We're each putting up a bottle of good liquor. We figure we'll need it after the announcement, no matter who it is."

That really made her laugh. "Good thinking. I'll put up a bottle of good vodka."

Their conversation was interrupted by Bartlett exiting the building. He had his usual entourage with him, and she shivered again.

John stood off to one side out of camera view. She turned to scan the crowd and noticed an odd look on Stephen's face. She wanted to ask him about it, but the governor began to speak.

"Ladies and gentlemen, thank you for coming out in this miserable weather. I will make this short, and we can move into the rotunda for some refreshments." He coughed.

"It has been a very difficult task to find a replacement for our former lieutenant governor, James Battelle. It was a long process and I am pleased to announce the new lieutenant governor is Senator Mike Hampton."

There was muffled applause because the entire audience was wearing winter gloves. Richard shook his head. "Told ya, Bartlett wants a rubber stamp for his agenda, and he couldn't have picked a better one. The man's lips have been glued to his ass for the last four years."

Ashley tried not to laugh out loud. The cameras were rolling, and the last thing she needed was to be caught on tape laughing at the governor's announcement.

Hampton came to the microphone. "I'll keep my remarks short, so we don't all freeze to death." That brought laughter from the audience.

"I consider it a great honor to be chosen for this spot. Jim Battelle left some very big shoes to fill, and I will do my best to fill them. I am humbled and honored to be chosen by Governor Bartlett and will work closely with him on projects to improve the great state of Idaho. Thank-you all for coming out today, and please join us in the rotunda for some refreshments."

The crowd broke up, with most heading into the capitol building. The news reporters joined the others while the camera crews headed back to their trucks.

Richard turned to the others. "Come on, let's head over to the bar. I've ordered pizza to be ready for us. We'll have enough time to have a decent lunch before the session starts this afternoon and we don't have to break bread with Bartlett or watch Hampton schmoozing up to the reporters like he's trying to sell them a '46 Chevy with no engine."

Marion frowned. "It's snowing lightly now, but if we go to the bar for lunch, we'll have to walk back on slippery streets."

Richard smiled. "Don't worry, Marion. I thought of that. Two of my waitresses drive minivans. I'll have them take us back to the capitol after we've eaten. They can drop us off at the back, and we can walk right into the building."

Marion smiled and nodded. No one else spoke on the walk to the bar. The wind picked up and blew snow in their faces. They were all rather stiff by the time they opened the front door.

The bar was quite toasty with a bright fire flickering in the big fireplace. A table in the back corner was ready for them with water pitchers, plates, napkins, and flatware.

As soon as they removed all of their hats and coats, they each found a seat at the table.

One of the waitresses came up. "The pizzas are coming out of the oven now. Would anyone like a salad to go with the pizza?" Ashley, Marion, and Stephen raised their hands.

Another waitress came up with a notepad. "What would you like to drink?" She took their orders, and no sooner had she left the table than the first waitress was back with the salads. The pizza and drinks arrive shortly after that, and everyone proceeded to fill their plates.

Marion placed a slice of pepperoni on her plate. "I'm not sure whether I should eat it or hold my hands over it for a while. I'm still freezing."

"Yeah, why did Bartlett hold the announcement outside in this weather? Wouldn't it have been better to move everything into the rotunda to start with?" Paul reached for the pizza.

"First, you can't do political announcements in the building, and second, he wanted the capitol building behind him when he made the announcement. It looks better on camera than being inside. People recognize the capitol immediately, and it looks very official. Most of the citizens in the state have never been inside it and have no idea what it looks like." Stephen poured dressing on his salad.

A waitress returned with chips, dip, and a small veggie tray. Paul and Frank immediately dug into those.

Stephen continued: "Setting up a press conference or announcement is more about the image you are trying to portray than what you actually say. When people see it on the news, a lot of times they are doing other things and only half-listening to what the speaker is saying. But the image of a man standing in front of the capitol building immediately lets the viewer know that this is an official announcement and gives off the feeling of authority and power. What the weather is in the shot is completely irrelevant."

"Boy, are you taking notes every time Mandy explains things to you?" Richard asked as he picked up his glass.

Stephen grinned. "Hey, the woman knows her stuff, and I'd be a fool not to listen to her when she speaks."

Other customers started filling the bar, and a few of the televisions on the far side of the room were turned on.

Frank set down his glass. "So he picked Hampton. I was hoping he'd go for someone we might be able to reason with, but you were right, he wanted someone completely loyal to his agenda."

"What did you think of all this, Ashley?" Marion asked.

"I wasn't surprised at all. When I had my interview with Bartlett…"

"You had an interview with Bartlett? When? Why didn't you tell us?" Stephen looked surprised.

"There wasn't much to talk about. He sent me a note with the meeting time last week, and he asked me a lot of questions. He wanted my opinion on different programs; some were his and some not. We talked about the economy and what could be done to help the state improve its business environment. He asked me several times about the use of state land by the land board and about what I thought of having federally managed lands within the state's borders. By the way, he's still fishing for who requested the data from all the different agencies."

Stephen and Richard nodded at each other and at Paul.

"It became clear after the first few minutes that I was part of the short list for window dressing at best or to try to turn me to his way of thinking at worst." She smiled at Richard. "I'd come to peace with the fact that I would not be chosen by him a while ago. Now that this is over with, I am looking forward to tweaking his nose when I sponsor the land bill in the senate."

Lunch continued with some discussion of two new bills that had been introduced in the house that morning. Everyone was well fed and watered by the time they had to return to the capitol.

Stephen walked into the historical society office and headed straight for the main desk. Tabitha saw him coming and stood up. "That was fast. I didn't expect you until tomorrow."

"You caught me at a good time. You found out who killed John Leeds?"

"Not exactly. The murderer was never caught, but I ran across a police report in the archives. The officer helped with the case and wrote extensive notes. He had suspicions about the case but could never prove them. He thought the murderer was Peter Van Buren in revenge for his daughter's death several years before."

Stephen could feel the color draining from his face. "Peter killed John?" This was something he could not tell his wife.

Richard closed his front door and dropped his keys in the crystal bowl on the entry table. He could hear his housekeeper puttering in the kitchen. The smell of roasting meat and spices came wafting from the same direction.

He hung up his coat and scarf in the closet and headed for the dining room.

"Mrs. Holcomb, what is that amazing feast I smell?"

"Mr. Fowler, it's *veneto* chicken. Now, get cleaned up and ready for supper."

Richard laughed. "Mrs. Holcomb, you always make me feel like I'm six years old and in trouble."

Mrs. Holcomb came out of the kitchen holding a wooden spoon. "Mr. Fowler, with half of the things you do, I think of you as being six years old. And as to trouble, well, it's attracted to you like iron shavings to a magnet." She gave him a warm smile. "I'll bring out the food; you get ready to eat."

A few minutes later, Richard sat at the table spooning chicken onto his plate. Mrs. Holcomb joined him after bringing in a basket of rolls.

He took a bite and closed his eyes. "Mrs. Holcomb, you are truly a goddess in the kitchen."

"Thank you, Mr. Fowler, but you say that with every meal."

"That's because it's always true." He took another bite. "Did you get the note I left you."

"It was hard to miss, being taped to the front of the microwave. When is your sister expected to arrive?"

"Sometime in the afternoon on Thursday, and she's leaving the next morning. It's a short stay, thank goodness. We still have all those empty liquor bottles in the garage?" He took a sip from his wine glass.

"Of course. I've wanted to throw them out. What do you want to do with them?"

"Tomorrow, I'd like you to go to the liquor store and pick up some bottles of cheap brandy, bourbon, vodka, gin, whiskey, and rum. We'll put the cheap stuff in the empty bottles of the expensive brands and put them in the liquor cabinet. Take all my good liquor and hide it in my bedroom closet."

"Don't you think Mr. Chip will know the difference?"

"Not the way he drinks. You could probably put cough syrup in those bottles. As long as it has a high enough alcohol content, he'll guzzle down anything. I'm not wasting good liquor on that sponge. That brings me to the next problem. Anything we have of value that can easily be pocketed needs to be taken down and put away. I don't think Lizzy would take anything, but I can't be sure.

I know Chip will pocket anything that isn't nailed down and with a good sturdy nail."

"Do you want me to bury the family silver?"

Richard grinned. "Oh, what a good idea. Do you think we can eat on paper plates with plastic utensils while they're here?"

"That's not a very nice way to treat your only sister."

"I don't care if it's nice. I don't want my grandmother's expensive antiques ending up at a swap meet in Arizona just to keep Chip in booze." He took another sip of wine. "Seriously, Mrs. Holcomb, you know my sister only shows up when she needs money. I just want a short pleasant dinner with her and the drunk, and then I want to ship them off in the morning without further losses.

"Is she bringing her son? He's the one I suspect made off with your grandmother's broach and the silver locket."

"She didn't mention him. I suspect he'll be staying in Arizona at a friend's house because it is a school night. Oh, and I invited Ashley Halliday to come to dinner that evening as well. I hope she'll be a positive influence and offer me some protection from my sister."

Mrs. Holcomb laughed. "If I didn't know better, I'd swear you two were adopted. You're nothing alike."

"Maybe I can tell Ashley that after she meets Liz. Otherwise, she might not want to go out with me again if she thinks it's hereditary."

Mrs. Holcomb grinned. "I'll make sure the house is secure, and I'll have a good meal ready for you and your guests."

"Thank you, Mrs. Holcomb. You truly are a jewel."

156

Chapter 22

Strange Dinner

The usual members of the group wandered into the small meeting room in the house's office wing. The smell of food filled the air as Richard unpacked the boxes from his bar.

Marion sat down in a chair. "Richard, you're a lifesaver. I'm starving."

"It's my pleasure, Marion. Here is your salad."

Stephen was the last one through the door. He locked it behind him.

Richard grinned. "Well, it looks like all the usual suspects are here. Let's get started."

Everyone got their lunches and took their seats.

Richard reached into his briefcase and pulled out a stack of paper. "Okay, this is a copy of the finished bill that I will give to the chairman of State Affairs Committee tomorrow. It calls for all federally administered lands within the borders of the state to be returned to state control and instructs the attorney general to file suit if the feds don't comply. It cites the equal footing law and what piss-poor managers the feds have been. Thanks to Paul and his brother, we have an amazing pile of evidence to back up our accusations. I'm giving the chairman only the bill tomorrow. He'll get to see the evidence when the rest of the committee sees it on Monday."

Frank held up his hand. "I have one question. How did you get the chairman to agree to keep quiet about the bill and let you present it without the usual process?"

Richard laughed. "By knowing something that no one else knows."

Stephen set down his sandwich. "Okay, Richard, spill."

"The chairman of the State Affairs Committee will be announcing in two weeks that he is running for the position of lieutenant governor of the state of Idaho."

"What?" Marion almost dropped her water bottle.

Stephen laughed. "Well, well, Bartlett is going to have a fit when he hears this. Your chairman has a good shot at winning. Hampton is pretty much disliked by everyone. Bartlett will have to help him raise money from his own list and have them run as a team if he wants to keep Hampton after the next election. That is assuming that he hangs on to his own seat, which I am working hard to take from him."

There was laughter and applause from the group.

Marion asked. "Frank, what is going on with your bill?"

Frank grinned. "Good news. It passed the committee this morning and is moving on to the house floor."

Richard held up his water bottle in a salute. "Well done, Frank. This is will hit Bartlett from both sides and shine the light on what he's really doing."

Paul set down his fork. "So what's the next step?"

Richard drank some water before answering. "I present the bill to the committee on Monday along with all the research. I make the motion to move the bill to printing. Stephen will second the bill, and the committee will discuss the matter. After about forty-five minutes of discussion, Stephen will call for the question, and we'll have a vote to shut off debate. When that passes, we'll vote on moving the bill forward. Then the fun begins as we round up votes to get it to pass on the house floor."

Marion frowned. "Why isn't Ashley here? Is someone else going to be the senate sponsor?"

"Ashley is actually having lunch with the chairman of the State Affairs Committee in the senate. She's laying the groundwork to make sure the bill gets brought up in committee for a vote when she presents it, and it's not just stuck on the chairman's desk and forgotten." Richard took a bite of his sandwich.

"She's not telling him about the bill is she?" Marion looked worried.

"No, she's just having lunch with him and a few other friendly senators to build up a relationship. This way, when she presents the bill, the chairman won't spike it." Richard checked his watch. "I need to get going. I have to meet with someone before the session starts. Enjoy lunch everyone, and I'll see you in the afternoon session."

Ashley parked her car in Richard's driveway. She'd no sooner stepped out of the car when the door opened and Richard came out.

"Thank God you're here. You have to save me from my family before I kill them or myself."

"Oh come on, it can't be that bad." She walked up to him and slid her arms around his waist.

"Well, maybe not that bad, but close." He gave her a kiss and then led her into the house. "At least Mrs. Holcomb is still here to clean up any spilled blood."

Ashley laughed. "Well, I'm looking forward to meeting your family and your housekeeper."

"Okay, but don't say I didn't warn you." He helped her with her coat. "Everyone is in the dining room. Come on." He took her hand and walked her into the room.

Elizabeth wasn't anything like she expected. Where Richard stood nearly six feet tall with thick, brown hair, his sister was barely over five feet with white-blonde hair. She reminded Ashley of a fairy. The only thing missing was her wings. In contrast, her husband looked like he belonged on the cover of Golf Digest, wearing off-white slacks and a peach polo shirt.

"Oh, Richard, she's beautiful." Liz came straight up to Ashley and took her right hand. She flipped it over and ran a finger over the lines. Something she saw there made her frown. She looked up and stared into Ashley's eyes. "You've been touched by darkness."

"Liz." Richard sounded angry. "I told you not to start this nonsense. I want a pleasant dinner and no silly supernatural talk. I mean, for heaven's sake, I haven't even introduced you yet."

"Well, Richard, there's no need for that. You told me you had invited your girlfriend Ashley over for dinner, and I'm sure you told her all the nasty stories about me and Chip, so we all know each other." She pulled Ashley's hand. "Come and sit down; I want to hear all about how you met my brother."

Ashley looked at Richard, who just shrugged his shoulders. This was definitely going to be a strange dinner.

Liz seated Ashley at the table and slipped into the seat next to her. "So, how did you meet my brother?"

"We met in politics. We were introduced by a mutual friend."

"Really, I told Richard he'd meet his next wife through politics. I read it in the cards." She turned to her brother. "Richard, why don't you get her a drink while we talk?"

"Ashley, a glass of wine?"

"Sure."

"A wine drinker like me. We are going to get along just fine." She picked up a large glass of wine and practically drained it in one gulp.

Chip chose that moment to lean over. "Hi, I'm Chip."

The alcohol fumes from his breath nearly knocked Ashley off her chair. The man wasn't just pickled, he was downright embalmed.

Richard returned with her glass of wine and gave her hand a quick squeeze of support. He wasn't kidding when he said his sister was a fruit loop and her husband a drunk.

"Sis, why don't you tell Ashley what you do in Arizona."

"My brother thinks I'm strange. I have a small shop, and I do massage therapy, aromatherapy, some palmistry, and card reading."

Richard lifted his glass of whiskey and saluted her.

"Don't be an ass, Richard. You spend your days playing in politics and running a bar."

Chip held up his glass. "I'm a golf pro." He drained the glass and picked up a bottle of bourbon and filled it again.

Mrs. Holcomb picked that moment to come in the door. "I have some appetizers for everyone." She set down a large platter with baked ravioli, deep-fried zucchini chips, and bruschetta, with a large bowl of marinara dip in the center.

"Mrs. Holcomb, allow me to introduce Ashley Halliday. Ashley, my wonderful housekeeper, Mrs. Holcomb who keeps me fed, watered, and in general repair."

Ashley gave the older woman a warm smile that was answered in kind.

"I'm delighted to finally meet you," Ashley said. "The Christmas dinner you made was absolutely delicious."

"It was my pleasure. I love to cook." She turned to Richard. "Dinner will be ready in about fifteen minutes."

"Thank you, Mrs. Holcomb." He looked back at the table. "Why don't we all sit down and start in on the food. Sis, you're over here next to Chip. I'll sit next to Ashley."

Everyone took their places. Richard grabbed a stack of plates from the sideboard and set them on the table. Chip immediately grabbed one and started loading it with food.

"That reminds me, Richard. Do you still have all that exercise equipment set up somewhere? Since Chip can't go running in the morning, he's going to need to do a gym workout."

Ashley nodded. So that's how the man kept looking trim and fit with all his drinking; he burned it off with exercise.

"The equipment is in the downstairs bedroom, the one with the large bay window that looks out on the backyard."

Chip got up and refilled his glass with whiskey and ice this time. He also brought over a bottle of wine and set it in front of his wife. Liz filled her large wine glass again. Ashley had always thought Richard was a heavy drinker, but compared to his sister and her husband, he was practically a teetotaler.

"What do you do besides politics, Ashley?" Liz took another gulp of wine.

"I have my own interior design company." She took a sip from her own glass.

"I could tell you were creative. It's in your aura."

"Liz." Richard gave her a glance.

Mrs. Holcomb came out with a large bowl of salad.

"Can I help with anything, Mrs. Holcomb?" Ashley wanted to get out of the room for a minute and away from Richard's sister. The woman kept staring at her, and it was downright creepy.

"Oh no dear, I can manage." Mrs. Holcomb disappeared back into the kitchen and reappeared again carrying two platters, of one of vegetables and the other of pasta. By the time she'd finished there were plates of chicken and beef, along with several different sauces. Chip began heaping food on his plate, and the rest followed his example with more moderation.

The conversation stopped while everyone ate. Liz kept glancing up at Ashley and frowning. After a while she set her fork down and just stared.

Ashley shivered. *What was wrong with this woman?*

"Ashley, you have been touched by evil. I can see it clearly."

"Liz." Richard dropped his knife on his plate with a clang.

"Richard, I can see it in her colors. Ashley, have you met someone recently who really made you feel uncomfortable?"

"Yes, Liz, she has. You." Richard glared at his sister.

"No, Richard, this is different. Look at her eyes. She has met someone. Ashley?"

"Well, now that you mention it, I have met someone who makes me feel defensive."

Richard looked up, his eyes widening. "Who?"

"That guy from the governor's office."

"The one you danced with at the ball?"

"Yes. He seemed nice at first, but now he just gives me the creeps." Ashley hurriedly picked up her wine glass and took a sip.

Richard felt the hair on the back of his neck stand up. His sister might be a flake, but when it came to her sensing things, well, she was right more than she was wrong. He didn't know how she did it. When they were children, she could look at a person and know things about them. He made fun of her at first, but when she kept hitting the mark with her observations, he learned not to dismiss them so quickly.

John Leeds, why did that man bother him as well? Time to give Jason a call and find out if there was anything to report about the man.

His sister was a nuisance, but she and her drunken husband would be gone in the morning. John, however, worked in Bartlett's office. That made Richard very uneasy.

He glanced around the table. Better find a safer topic of discussion.

"So, Chip, have you been following basketball this season?

Chapter 23
Questions

Bill McCreary, the chairman of the State Affairs Committee, had a private office on the second floor of the capitol building. Richard arrived shortly after six thirty in the morning and called McCreary's office every five minutes until the chairman answered his phone at ten minutes after seven.

"I have the bill for you. Are you alone up there? I really don't want anyone to notice our private meeting."

"No one is here yet, Richard. If you come up now, it should be safe."

"Good, on my way." Richard hung up the phone and grabbed the folder on his desk. He took to back stairs to avoid being seen. Bartlett had spies and flunkies all over the building, and he was sure someone would tell the governor about his meeting with McCreary. Bartlett knew someone had requested the land data, and it wouldn't take the man long to figure out who, if he was seen with the chairman of the State Affairs Committee. Bartlett was a lot of things, but stupid wasn't one of them.

When he reached the door to the second floor, Richard had to wait in the stairwell before coming out. Two pages were in the hallway holding a conversation, and he knew that some of the pages couldn't be trusted. The line from that movie came back to him, the one about not just being paranoid, but whether he was paranoid enough. When it came to Bartlett and his underhanded tactics, there was no such thing as too much caution.

McCreary was pacing his office when Richard arrived. Richard closed the door, locked it, and lowered the blinds.

"That bad is it?" McCreary asked.

"For Bartlett it is." He handed over the folder.

"Have a seat." McCreary motioned to one of the guest chairs in front of his desk. He read the bill as he walked around to the other side and then dropped into his chair.

"You have got to be kidding me. You really want to present this bill?" The chairman shook his head. "I must be out of my mind to allow this."

Richard grinned. "You're not out of your mind. And since you're planning on challenging Hampton in the next primary, you need something like this to make a big headline splash."

"Why do you think the committee would ever vote this out onto the floor? I mean the cost of taking over the federal land has got to be considerable. The taxpayers will never understand it or stand for it."

"They will when they see all the evidence that backs up my position."

McCreary shifted in his chair. "So you're the one who's been collecting all the data from the different departments. I had one of Bartlett's staffers in here asking me about it. So why this bill and why now?"

Richard relaxed a little. "Believe it or not, it's all about education funding."

"Really? How so?"

"Bartlett is trying to get the state involved in the federal Enhanced Education Plan. That will take away local control over education. He wants to use the federal grant money for schools and reduce the state's contribution so he can shift the money to some of his own projects. He will have the education board change over from paper textbooks to tablets and laptops. The savings from this will go to teacher's salaries, and in return he'll get their support for the Enhanced Education Plan. A nice piece of political sleight of hand, until the grant money dries up and the taxpayers are left holding the bag. Then they have to pay for the increased federal mandates, over which they have no say, plus bear the increases in property taxes to cover the daily operations costs that the state used to pay for. You know as well as I do that once the state funds a project, it is almost impossible to take the money away. This way, Bartlett can shift state money to the projects he wants to fund but can't get through the legislature on a straight vote. By the time the grant money runs out, he'll be out of office, and the next governor will have to deal with the angry voters."

McCreary shook his head. "Wow, you really know how to rain on Bartlett's parade. Do you think Hampton is aware of this?"

"I'd be stunned if he wasn't. He's been Bartlett's hatchet man for years, and now he's the lieutenant governor. I'd say he's in this up to his eyeballs."

"Can I use this in my campaign against Hampton?"

Richard smiled. "Absolutely, but not until after I present the bill on Monday."

"Okay, what do you need from me?"

"Don't schedule anything else for Monday's committee meeting. The presentation and debate for this bill will take the whole session. I will have copies of the bill for each of the committee members plus the two needed for the record. I'll have copies of the research data for everyone as well. I kid you not; the stack of papers each person will receive is five inches tall. I'm having everything printed offsite so there will be no leaks. You know as well as I do, if I have the legislative printing services prepare this stuff, it will be in Bartlett's office as fast as it takes someone to get from the basement to the second floor."

"You, amaze me, Richard. You paid for all this research and printing yourself didn't you."

"Yes, and it's not exactly something I can claim on my taxes. Do you have any other questions before I sneak out of here?"

"No." He took the bill and slid it into his briefcase. "I won't let this out of my sight until the committee meeting. Watch your back; Bartlett is going to blow a gasket when he finds out what you've done."

Richard gave him a wide grin showing his teeth. "I'm counting on it."

Richard picked up the blinking phone on his desk in the house chamber. "Yes,"

"I want to present a bill that bans any more special license plates."

Richard grinned. "I'll co-sponsor it. I'm pretty sure we can get unanimous consent from the body as well." He looked over at Stephen and saw his shoulders shake.

"One of these days one of us is going to laugh out loud at the jokes we tell during the session, and we'll both be in trouble with the Speaker." Richard picked up his pen.

"If it happens, I'm sure it will be your fault."

"Stephen, are you free for drinks after the session?"

"Yes, Rose has a late fitting for a wedding dress. It's amazing how many weddings happen on Valentine's Day. What time?

"I'll meet you at my bar at five thirty."

"See you then."

John stood in the corridor outside of the house offices. He still couldn't figure out what happened during his dream of walking with Ashley. She shouldn't have woken up like that. He cracked his knuckles. If he couldn't enter Ashley's dreams, maybe a more direct approach would work. He'd confront the man who stole his wife. Pacing back and forth in front of the security guard at the desk, he kept thinking of what to say to Winship. At least he wouldn't be with his friend; the one who wanted Ashley. John had come around the corner in time to see him leave with two other people. If another man was after one of his old girlfriends, he'd enlighten him very quickly about the situation and tell the man to leave what's his alone. Nobody touched anything that was his without his permission.

The door opened, and Winship walked out. John stepped forward and saw the spark of recognition in Winship's eyes. Good, no need for social pleasantries then.

"I'd like to speak to you."

"You and I have nothing to say to each other." Winship continued walking.

"Oh, I think we have plenty to say to one another."

The security guard rose from his seat.

Stephen stopped and glanced in the guard's direction and then back at John.

"I am not interested in speaking to you, and that goes for your boss, too." Stephen turned and walked away.

Richard sat in the corner at a table with a glass of whiskey going over the grocery order for the bar. He glanced at his watch. Stephen was late.

It took another fifteen minutes before his friend came in, looking a bit flustered.

He waved Stephen over.

"You look like you could use a good stiff drink."

Stephen took a seat. "No, I have to drive home. I'll just have a beer."

"Okay." Richard signaled to one of the waitresses.

"So, why are you late?"

Stephen unbuttoned his coat and draped it over the chair. "I got stopped in the hall by one of Bartlett's staffers."

Richard raised an eyebrow. "John Leeds by any chance?" The look on his friend's face told him all he needed to know. "What is the matter with that guy?"

"Oh, nothing, he's just one of Bartlett's toadies." Stephen wouldn't look up from the table.

Richard scoffed. "He's a lot more than that. I saw the look on Rose's face at the Governor's Ball. She was absolutely terrified."

"A misunderstanding, she thought he was somebody else," Stephen said.

Richard narrowed his eyes. Stephen was keeping something from him, and that wasn't like Stephen at all. There was something odd about John Leeds, and Stephen wouldn't talk about it.

"Stephen, don't ever play poker; you don't have the face for it."

The waitress came up. "Misty, bring Stephen a Bud Light, and is my food order ready?"

"It's coming up now, boss. I'll bring it over with the beer."

When she left the table, he looked at his friend. "Stephen, if you don't want to tell me about John, that's fine. I'll do my own research. Now, let's get down to business. Let me tell you what happened with the chairman..."

Stephen walked into his house. "Rose, are you home?"

There was no answer. He checked his watch, fifteen minutes after seven. She could be home any minute. He hung up his coat and scarf and went over to the sofa. He sat down and started to speak. "Gabriel, I need to talk to you."

It took a few minutes, but a bright light shone behind him.

"I'm here, Stephen. I'm listening."

"He came to me, Gabriel. My best friend and I couldn't warn him. I made the only decision I could. I will not lose my wife. But why do I have to make that choice? Why can't I warn Richard? He already knows the truth about Rose. John was an arrogant, self-centered prick when he was alive; I'm sure he hasn't improved much after rotting in a grave for over a hundred years. He's going to hurt Richard, or Ashley, or Rose; I know it, and I'm helpless to do anything about it." Stephen buried his face in his hands.

"And how would you stop John if you had an opportunity?" The light grew brighter, and he heard material rustling.

"I don't know, hit him, I suppose. If he can walk around and interact with people, that means he's solid, if only temporarily. If he's solid, then I can hurt him."

"You'd be arrested for assault, and where would that get you?"

Stephen heard the angel move again. "I don't know. I just feel like I need to do something."

"You are doing something by taking care of your wife and your unborn child. You are running for governor and will be able to do a lot of good if you succeed and win the election. Believe it or not, those are the most important things you can do right now."

"But what about Richard and Ashley?"

"It is admirable that you care so much for your friends, but know this; I care for them too. Stephen, you are witnessing things that are beyond you, like the stars are beyond the earth. Most people go through their entire lives ignorant of the things you have seen. Perhaps it is better that way, but that time has passed for you. You are a part of this now, a pawn on the chessboard. Most people, when they play chess, they watch the larger pieces closely, the sly bishops, the solid castles, the skillful knights, and the treacherous queen. Most people don't pay any attention to the lowly pawns, well, not after the first moves anyway. They are considered by many to be throwaway pieces, sacrifices on the board for a larger purpose. But a pawn can attack the king the same way as the other pieces on the board. Using pawns to their greatest potential is my specialty. Just because you don't see me moving mountains or smiting someone with lightning doesn't mean that I am idle. Trust me, Stephen. Follow my instructions, and I will see you and yours safely to the other side." The light faded, and Stephen sat alone in his living room.

Chapter 24
More Questions

Richard had the pages place the boxes on the floor. He'd made sure each one was taped shut, so no one could see what was inside or take out any of the contents. None of Bartlett's people was present yet, but the moment he presented his bill, someone would be sent to try to persuade the committee to vote against it. His money was on Hampton or Radnor.

The committee members slowly entered the room. McCreary came in and called the meeting to order. After a few normal business procedures, the chairman called on Richard.

"Mr. Chairman, I would like to present a bill for this committees' approval on reclaiming Idaho land from the federal government."

There was a murmur around the table and Richard opened the first box, pulling out copies of his bill.

Stephen watched his friend's performance and noted the expressions on all the faces of the committee members. They ran the gamut from hostility, skepticism, astonishment, and curiosity to approval. He continued to watch as Richard brought out each stack of research evidence to support his position. One by one, the faces around the table changed and Stephen calculated how the vote would go. Somewhere in the middle of the presentation, Radnor came into the room and took a seat along the back wall among the lobbyists and other guests. By the time Richard pulled out the summary sheet, Radnor was the color of custard pudding. Stephen smiled. Bartlett was going to have kittens over this bill.

The discussion phase of the process began and consisted mostly of questions about the data and the cost of taking over management of the land. Richard made it clear; the upfront costs were high, but in the long run the state would make up the initial expense and have a new, continuing source of revenue. The discussion continued on for over an hour until Stephen called for the question. The final vote was three opposed and eight in favor of sending it on for a vote by the full house.

Radnor left the room as soon as the vote was taken. Stephen leaned back in his chair, wondering if the governor would swear loud enough to be heard up here on the third floor.

Ashley stood on the main floor of the capitol rotunda, waiting for Richard and Stephen to leave the house wing of the building. After a while she was joined by Marion, Frank, and Paul, each just as anxious as she was to find out what had happened.

Frank stared at the elevator. "Do you think Bartlett had them assassinated?"

Ashley shuddered.

Marion frowned. "Frank, that's not funny."

Paul tapped Frank on the shoulder. "They're coming, look." He pointed to the stairs leading to the senate side of the building. Everyone turned in the direction he pointed.

When they reached the bottom of the stairs, Ashley came over and took Richard's hand. "Why are you coming that way?"

"Radnor and Hampton were camped in the hallway on the house side. We went down the back stairs and came around to the senate side so we wouldn't be detained or questioned." Richard squeezed her hand.

"Richard caused enough of a stir this morning. We thought it better to make ourselves scarce." Stephen wrapped a scarf around his neck.

"On that note, let's head over to the bar for lunch. I think it might be prudent to get out of this building and get in front of some neutral witnesses." Richard led the way out of the door.

A short while later, they all sat at their regular table in the corner of Richard's bar.

Paul held up his glass of coke. "I'd like to salute the man of the hour, Richard Fowler."

A chorus of hear, hear, came from around the table.

"I consider it a great honor to be an official thorn in the governor's side." Richard held up his own glass of ginger ale.

"So, what's the next move?" Paul asked.

"Theoretically, it goes to the house for a first reading on the calendar, but I'd be a fool if I didn't expect Bartlett to try to stick a wrench in the works somewhere along the line." Richard set his glass down.

"I don't think we'll have to wait long for him to make a move. He wants the grant money after all and having the state hand the federal government eviction papers is not the way to build a warm relationship." Stephen picked up his sandwich.

Frank looked at his watch. "We'd best head back. The afternoon session is starting in half an hour.

On the walk back, Ashley pulled Richard aside. "I've been thinking. I'd like you to meet my parents."

"Really, hmm, I'm not sure your father is going to like me any better than he liked Stephen. Don't forget, I've already been divorced twice. That is not an endearing trait to most fathers."

"That's why I thought we should do this on neutral ground."

"What, meet in a church?"

"No, silly, I'm going to talk to Morgan and Ann Tate and see if they will host a dinner for my folks and us." Ashley pulled up the collar of her coat against the wind.

"That might work; at least Morgan knows my family well and could put in a good word for me. Let me know if he'll do it."

Richard picked up the phone and dialed Jason. He settled into a more comfortable position on the sofa and put his feet up on the ottoman. Jason answered on the third ring.

"Hello, Richard. I take it you've read it?"

"Yes, I have, and it's a little light on substance."

Richard looked over at the report from Jason's office and frowned. Normally the reports were complete with dates and surveillance locations. This one, well, to put it mildly, was as solid as Swiss cheese. It showed several brief sightings of John at the capitol and at one or two at different political functions but nothing else.

"Where does he live?"

"That's why I sent it over to you early. I can't seem to find out. The guy just disappears and shows up again the next morning."

"That doesn't make any sense. He has to live somewhere." Richard shifted his position on the sofa.

"I'm telling you, I can't find out where. His name isn't on any lease company list that I can find or on the county property tax rolls. I suppose he could live with a relative or friend but we haven't actually seen him leaving the capitol and heading anywhere. And that brings up another issue; apparently he's working as an intern because his name does not appear on the governor's payroll."

"Hmm…well the man needs to eat so he's getting money or support from somewhere." Richard scratched his chin. "If he's an intern, then he's being sponsored by one of the universities."

"I know; I've checked with all the state's colleges and universities, and there is no record of him attending any of them. Are you sure you have the right name?"

"That was the name he gave Ashley Halliday." Richard was getting a very uneasy feeling about this.

"Maybe she misunderstood him. I can do a search for names that are close to Leeds.

"Go ahead. I want to find out who this guy is and why he's here. Call me when you've found something."

"Will do."

"Thanks, Jason." Richard hung up the phone, curiosity and suspicion warring for the top slot in his thoughts. He had a very odd feeling that no matter where Jason searched, he wouldn't come up with any more information on John Leeds.

He stared at the small fire in his fireplace. Rose recognized the man at the ball. Perhaps it was time to make a private visit to the angel statue in the cemetery.

Chapter 25

Puzzle Pieces

"How in the hell did we not see this coming?" Bartlett stomped around the room.

Radnor leaned back in his chair. When his boss was on a rant like this, the best thing to do was sit quiet and let him get it out of his system.

"We knew someone had requested the fire data on state land adjoining federal. Why didn't we put two and two together?" Bartlett dropped into his desk chair.

Mason noticed the pale look of Bartlett's skin and the shine of perspiration on his forehead. Bartlett's health was beginning to worry him.

"The bill is sponsored by Fowler, but I'll bet Winship is behind it. He thinks he can take me out next year by having another issue to the debate me on." He picked up his pen and tapped it on the desk. "All right, so what do we do now?"

Mason shifted his position. "We start by calling in some of our markers from the different house members we've done favors for. The easiest thing would have been to kill it in committee, but we're too late for that."

"And how did that happen? We should have heard about the bill being proposed. How was Fowler able to keep it under wraps until he presented it before the committee?" Bartlett pulled out a handkerchief and started wiping his face.

"There's only one way to pull that off and that is with the cooperation of the chairman. Which brings up the question of why would the chairman of the State Affairs Committee want this bill to make it through the committee? I think we need to keep an eye on McCreary. I expect there was some sort of quid pro quo involved."

Bartlett reached into his jacket pocket and pulled out a pill. He stuck it in his mouth and reached for the water glass. "What I want to know from you is way didn't you tell me as soon as you found out about it yesterday?"

Mason wrinkled his forehead. "I went to find you but ran into Sarah instead. She told me you were at the doctor's office and wouldn't be available until this morning."

"My wife isn't the governor, and she doesn't pay your salary. When something like this happens, I expect you to let me know immediately."

Mason raised an eyebrow. "You are telling me to defy Sarah? I'm sorry but I plan to live a while longer, and poking a tiger with a stick is not a way to achieve that goal."

Bartlett laughed. "No, I suppose not. Okay, what's happened has happened; what do we do to fix it?"

"Like I said before, we start calling in markers and rounding up votes against it." He reached into his shirt pocket and pulled out a small notebook and pen. "I will start making calls today and see how many I can line up."

"Why don't we tell the Speaker to pull the bill or not allow it to get on the calendar?" Bartlett took another sip from his water glass.

"If we try to get heavy-handed like that, we're likely to have a mutiny in the house and end up with the opposite effect, with everyone voting for the bill because they're angry. Not to mention handing Stephen Winship a prime campaign issue to beat you over the head with on the campaign trail. No, the best way is to line up a group in opposition and take it out on a floor vote." He scribbled in his notebook.

Bartlett snorted. "That didn't work out so well with the grocery tax bill last year, and we are up against the same team, I suspect."

"I'm sure you're right about that. Plus the amount of data that Fowler presented in support of his position was impressive."

Bartlett scoffed. "Fowler is nothing but a rich drunk, who plays at being a legislator to have something to do in the beginning of the year when the weather is bad."

"Russ, don't underestimate the man just because you don't like him. He may be rich and he may like his whiskey, but he's no fool. He did his homework on this one and we were caught flat-footed." He stood up and stuffed the pen and notebook back in his pocket. "I have to talk to a few reporters and see if I can spin the story so the public thinks this is a bad idea for the state. I'll be in my office if you need me."

Bartlett nodded. "I'll send a message to Hampton to get here as soon as the session is over. We might as well start working on the senate and make sure the bill gets stuffed in a drawer over there and never sees the light of day."

Richard glanced at the clock on the dashboard. He didn't have a lot of time for this little excursion. There was an event at the bar this evening, and he needed to be there to make sure things ran smoothly. The afternoon light was fading, and there wouldn't be another opportunity for this little trip.

Traffic was unusually snarled. It had snowed this morning, and not all the side streets were plowed. Cars traveled slowly, and it took several changes of the traffic lights before he could get through the various intersections. If it took much longer to get there, he'd have to break out his flashlight in order to walk around. At long last he turned onto Latah Avenue and drove to the entrance to Morris Hill Cemetery.

The cemetery road wasn't plowed, which didn't really surprise him. That's why he drove the SUV today with four-wheel drive. He went a short way along the road and stopped. He'd have to walk from here; it was time to change into his snow boots.

He walked along the snowy path trying not to step on any half buried headstones. This was actually the first time he'd come out to find the grave. He remembered Stephen's description of its location, and he had seen the pictures Jason had taken. It had to be around here somewhere. He walked around looking for a clump of fir trees. When he found her, a shiver ran down his spine. The angel statue stood inside a cluster of evergreens. She looked exactly like Rose Winship. He half-expected the statue to move. The sculptor who created her had used a portrait of Rose as his guide. The portrait currently hung in the Whitney Western Art Museum in Cody, Wyoming.

Richard walked up to the statue and bent down. The inscription was buried under the snow, and he had to dig a little to clear it. Stephen wouldn't discuss John, and Rose was clearly terrified of him. That could mean only one thing. He was someone she knew from before.

He scraped his hand along the base of the pedestal and scraped away the ice. He carefully read the words carved into the stone. "Rose Van Buren Leeds. Died of a broken heart. 1861–1882."

The date made his skin crawl. The woman had lived over a hundred and thirty years ago. Then he looked closely at the name and felt like someone had punched him in the gut. Leeds. Oh, sweet mercy, John was Rose's dead husband. The one responsible for her death.

All the way back to the bar, Richard ran the events of the last few weeks through his mind. He didn't know whether to be angry with Stephen for not telling him or grateful for keeping him out of this mess. Everything fell into place now. Rose's reaction to the man, Ashley's feeling of unease, Jason's inability to find out where he lived, even his sister's reaction to Ashley.

Why hadn't Stephen told him? He thought they were close friends. He couldn't believe that Stephen would do anything to hurt him. He should have said something. Stephen had him stand next to his wife at the announcement, for heaven's sake. Stephen didn't want Rose to be all alone and unprotected. Look at the money he was spending to put a security system in the dress shop and the private car service to pick her up and take her home. Stephen was doing everything he could to protect Rose. Maybe it wasn't that he wouldn't warn anyone about John. What if he couldn't. That made more sense. Stephen would do anything to protect his wife.

Richard sat at a light, running over everything again. He didn't have enough information about John in the past. Stephen wouldn't discuss the man, so that meant he needed another source of information. Rose would be able to tell him, but under the circumstances that was a bad idea. He scratched his chin.

The light changed and he moved again. He was almost at the bar, and there was nothing more he could do tonight. Tomorrow he'd make a few phone calls. Maybe the historical society would have the information he needed.

Chapter 26
Information

Rachel straightened her father's tie while Radnor handed the governor his list of talking points.

"Don't forget to mention the legislation you are supporting to help fund the schools."

"Mason, I can read, you know. Do we have some planted questions in the room? Rachel, sweetie, not too tight on the tie if you please; I don't want to start choking on camera. Be an angel and see if you can round up your mother. I'm going to need you both up front for this."

When Rachel left the room, Mason answered. "Yes, I contacted all our friendly reporters and made sure they each had a good question to ask. You are likely to get some hostile questions as well. I tried to limit the number of reporters in the room, but it's hard to keep out our enemies without being obvious about it. The last thing we need right now is an article about how we are manipulating the media and hiding the truth. Winship would jump on that in a heartbeat and milk it for all its worth. Mandy Sawyer is far too clever a political adviser to let something like that slide."

"Yeah, a pity she's not willing to work for us. There aren't many campaign managers of that quality around." Bartlett shifted in his chair.

"Well, I don't think she'll ever forgive you for pulling the funding out from under that congressional candidate she had a couple of years ago."

Bartlett snorted. "The man was loose cannon. We'd never have been able to control him. I'm glad he didn't make it. The one we have now is easy to work with and understands who helped him win." He grabbed a handkerchief and dabbed at his forehead.

Mason frowned. His boss really didn't look well. He'd have to have a private talk with Sarah and see if there was anything he could do to lighten the schedule or get the man to eat better. There wasn't a chance he could get Bartlett to do that without the help of his wife. The only person who could order him to do something and get away with it was Sarah.

"Russ, I'm going to send the makeup girl in here again. You've streaked some of your coloring. You don't want to look like a zebra on television."

Bartlett frowned but nodded.

Radnor slipped out and closed the door. "Sally, you need to redo the governor's makeup. I think he looks a bit pale, and I want more color in his face for the cameras. He looks like he's been hibernating all winter."

"I tried to do that before, but he wouldn't let me."

"Keep the makeup box behind him so he can't see what colors you're using and make sure he has good color in his cheeks. If he asks you anything about it, just lie and say it's exactly what you did last time and you wouldn't have to do it again if he hadn't smeared it."

"Yes, sir." She picked up her box and went back in the room.

Radnor saw Rachel coming around the corner. She smiled when she saw him.

"Mom's right behind me. She got stopped in the hall by someone, but she'll be here in a minute." As she spoke, Sarah came around the corner.

Sarah might stand a little over five feet in height but had a spine of steel. "I've been in the gold room making sure everything is ready for the press conference. Most of the reporters are there. The ones who are missing are caught up in traffic due to the slick roads. I checked with their networks, and they will be here shortly. Why aren't you in there with him?"

"He's been mopping his face with his handkerchief and smeared his makeup. I just sent the girl in to freshen him up. Can I speak to you privately for a moment?"

Sarah nodded. "Rachel, will you go back upstairs and wait for us in the gold room? Don't answer any questions a reporter might ask you. Tell them that your dad will answer all of their question when he gets there."

Rachel looked disappointed but went down the hall.

"Sarah, is there something wrong with Russell? I mean his color looks bad, and he's constantly mopping sweat off his face."

Sarah pursed her lips. "This is to be held in the strictest confidence." She gave him a look that let him know in no uncertain terms that he'd be disemboweled if he breathed a word of this, and she'd be the one wielding the knife. "He is having problems with his heart. He is on new medication. He's very sensitive about this, so don't discuss it with him."

"Yes, ma'am. We should go in now. I expect he's ready." He held the door open for her.

Bartlett looked a lot better. Sally knew her craft. She closed her case and nodded as she left the room.

"Ready to face the jackals, Russ?"

"I'm not afraid. Sarah will protect me, won't you, dear?" He smiled at his wife.

"Come on, the late comers should be there by the time we arrive." Sarah patted his arm.

The gold room sat on the fourth floor of the capitol. It was a good-sized room and set up for press briefings. The chairs were all filled, and three cameramen stood in the back with their portable units on tripods. Rachel stood by herself in a corner.

Bartlett entered with his wife on his arm. He immediately started greeting the different reporters by name and joking with them.

Radnor shook his head. His boss was really part showman. He'd never seen a politician work the room like Russell Bartlett. Even those reporters who were not friendly to his administration, spoke with him and laughed at his jokes. Sarah walked over to her daughter and stood beside her.

When Bartlett finished schmoozing with everyone present, he took his place at the podium. "Thank you all for coming in this miserable weather. I'm thinking of introducing a bill next week to limit the snowfall to Bogus Basin ski resort so we can all drive safely down here."

That brought a good laugh. He continued on with his prepared speech, hitting on all the highlights of his past term in office and making sure he mentioned all the talking points Radnor had given him.

"So, I am officially announcing that I am running for a second term to continue the progress we have made in this state. Sarah, Rachel, can you come up and join me, please?" They both came up and stood on either side of him. He waved to the crowd and let the video and still camera operators get all the angles they needed. When the photo op was finished, the two women went back to their corner and Bartlett stepped up to the microphone. "I'll entertain some questions from the floor."

He answered many questions about different policies and the future economy of the state. A woman in the middle of the pack raised her hand and he called on her. "Yes, Lacy, you have a question?"

Radnor was leaning against the wall but stood up now. Lacy Baker, a small blonde with a pinched nose like a ferret, was his go-to reporter. Anytime he wanted someone embarrassed or a story leaked, all he had to do was call, and she'd run with whatever he gave her.

"Governor Bartlett, I understand you are working hard to bring in some federal grants for education that will help improve funding without calling for a tax increase on our citizens. Can you elaborate on that?"

The perfect opening, a slow pitch right over the plate. Radnor leaned back against the wall. His trained reporter had delivered again.

Bartlett took several minutes to explain his plan and lay out the benefits for state education. When he finished answering, her hand shot up again. "A follow-up question, sir. I understand there are two bills making their way through the house that would stop your program from being implemented. The first is a bill requiring every local school board to approve the curriculum before it can be implemented. I understand that if any school boards opt out of the program, the grant money will be withheld. And the second bill calls for Idaho to take back control of state land currently administered by the federal government. This could also derail your program and withhold grant money. Can you elaborate on this as well?"

Mason grinned. The woman really knew how to deliver the low-hanging fruit.

Bartlett started in explaining how the curriculum was already vetted by the U.S. Department of Education, and having the local school boards review it was a waste of time and taxpayer money. Then he started in on the land bill and really got on a roll. He laid out the argument against state control, and explained the cost of such an idea and the ongoing problems that it would create.

Mason shook his head. Bartlett truly had the gift of political bullshit. The man could strip a person of his house and land and leave him feeling grateful that he was able to contribute to the cause. After today's press conference, Fowler was going to have a hard sell to get his bill through the legislature.

Richard hurried back to his desk in the house office wing. The whole building was buzzing about Bartlett's press conference. Clever of the old fox to do it while all the legislators were in committee meetings. This way no one with any knowledge could call him on his lies. He took a deep breath. There was no time to think about that problem now; he could deal with it later. He only had a small window of time to make a private call to the Idaho Historical Society, and he didn't want to miss the opportunity.

He would have preferred to drive down there and speak to someone in person, but with today's lousy weather, he'd never make it back in time for the afternoon session.

A woman picked up the phone on the third ring. "Hello, historical society."

"Hello, I'm looking for information about a man who lived in Boise in the 1800s. Is there someone I can talk to about this?"

"Well, sir. We have an extensive library of information, but it is by no means complete. Who is it that you are looking for?"

"A man by the name of John Leeds."

"That name doesn't ring any bells for me, but let me ask one of the other librarians. Tabitha, have you ever heard of a man from the 1800s named John Leeds?"

Richard could hear the woman answer in the background. "John Samuel Leeds or John Jacob Leeds?"

"I don't know."

"Let me have the phone; I'll talk to the caller."

The phone rattled, and another woman came on the line. "Can I help you?"

"Yes, I'm trying to find out information about John Leeds. It sounds like there were at least two men by that name. What do you know about them?" Richard shifted in his chair.

"Well, Mr. Leeds seems to be a popular fellow. I just finished doing research on John Jacob Leeds for someone else. Do you know which one you want?"

"Well, I'm not sure. Are the two men related?"

"Yes. John Samuel Leeds is the father. He built up quite a mining empire in the West from 1860 to 1895 but lost it all through mining strikes, shafts playing out, and some bad business decisions. He died at the age of sixty-eight, penniless."

Richard bit his lip. He wasn't quite sure how this whole ghost thing worked. Once you died did you come back at a younger age than when you died? Rose didn't. She died at twenty-one and came back at the same age. "I don't think that's the right one. The one I'm looking for was married to a woman named Rose."

"Oh, that's John Jacob Leeds, the son. The family sent him to Harvard to for his education, to groom him to take over the family business and to become the first governor when Idaho acquired statehood."

Richard nearly fell off his chair. "He was running for governor?"

"Well yes, but the scandal over his wife's death put an end to his plans."

"Scandal? What happened?"

"Apparently, she caught him with one of his mistresses and ran out into a storm. She caught pneumonia and died a few days later."

Richard slumped in his chair. Poor Rose, no wonder the sight of the man terrified her. "What else can you tell me about him?"

"He was the spokesman for the mining consortium that tried to delay statehood, and he was murdered on his way home from one of the local saloons."

Richard felt like someone had hit him with a brick. "Murdered? Do you know who did it?"

"No, the person was never caught. He was found lying in a small field near his home, stabbed in the back and a broken bottle of whiskey in his hand."

Richard stammered. "Thank you, ma'am. That's what I needed to know. Goodbye."

He hung up the phone and sat in the chair staring at the wall. Murdered, and now the man was back and working for Bartlett. Crap. He had to find a way to protect Ashley.

Chapter 27
Relatives

Richard dreaded making the phone call, but he really had nowhere else to turn. He checked his watch. If he could keep her from rambling, he'd have enough time to get the answers he needed and make it to the Tate's for dinner with Ashley's folks.

He stretched out on his sofa, made a silent prayer for strength and patience, and then dialed his sister.

She answered on the first ring. "I knew you'd be calling me. I did a card reading this morning. They showed me you were greatly disturbed, so what's the problem?"

He cleared his throat. "Liz, how do you defend someone from a ghost?"

"Oh, gracious, it's Ashley isn't it? I could see something dark had touched her. Her colors were off and there was a gray area behind her eyes."

Richard heard the sound of books being dropped onto the floor from a height. "Sis, what are you doing?"

"I need to consult a book. Hang on a minute." There were more sounds of things falling and of ringing chimes.

"Found it. Do you know what type of ghost it is?"

"What do you mean what type of ghost it is? It's the spirit of someone who has died."

"Richard, spirits only come back for a reason. It takes a lot of energy to enter the land of the living from the spirit world. You just don't do that on a lark. Spirits can come back to help people or warn them. Evil spirits can come back because of jealousy, or anger, or trying to reach a goal they were denied in life. Do you know anything about the spirit?"

Richard frowned. "I know he was a selfish bastard in life. I doubt a hundred and twenty odd years have improved him any."

"The spirit is that old? Oh, that's bad. The older they are, the more energy they can hold and the longer they can plague the living." The sound of pages being flipped in rapid succession came over the phone. "Here it is. 'Time has a distilling effect on the dead. It causes them to acquire a sponge-like quality enabling the spirit to extract power from living beings and hold it in themselves, allowing them to be seen by the living or interact through dreams.'"

"Do you mean to tell me there are actual books about this stuff?"

"Oh Richard, don't you remember your Shakespeare? 'There are more things in heaven and earth, Horatio, than are dreamt of in your philosophy.' This stuff has always been around you, brother. But you, like most people, refuse to see it."

"How on earth did you get involved in this?" He rubbed his temple.

"Grandma. She was very much into the supernatural. You have all her stuff; didn't you ever read her diary or look at some of the books she had packed in that old trunk?"

"That stuff is all in storage, and I never go there. Now, back to the topic, what can I do to defend Ashley against this ghost?"

"Silver. And not just any type of silver. It needs to be dipped in holy water and blessed by a priest."

"Anything else?"

"Well, burning sage candles can disrupt their energy flow. Salt is a good barrier protection, but you have to place it in front of all openings, like thresholds, windowsills, or fireplaces."

"I can't exactly spread salt all around her apartment. Her neighbors will have a fit. Besides, she's gone a lot. A personal defense that she can keep on her at all times is best."

"Well, that brings us back to silver. A piece of silver jewelry like a ring or a necklace would work well."

"I'm meeting her for dinner in an hour. I don't have enough time to find a priest, let alone one who's willing to bless a piece of jewelry for me without calling the cops." He ran his fingers through his hair.

"You don't have to. You have all of Grandma's things, right?"

"Yes, why?"

"Where is her jewelry box? The small, wooden one with the cracked mirror in the lid?"

"Upstairs in the attic."

"Find the box and open it. There is a necklace in there. A small dragonfly made of sapphires. The wings and the chain are silver. Remember, she wore it all the time around Halloween. She had it dipped in holy water and blessed by a priest. She wore it every time she felt uneasy. Find the necklace and give it to Ashley. Tell her to wear it and not take it off until the ghost is gone."

"Liz, she doesn't know about the ghost, and I'm not sure I want her to."

"It will be harder to protect her if she doesn't understand the need for it."

"I know, but I think if she finds out, I'm not sure she can handle it. Thanks, sis. I owe you one."

"Yes, you do, and you know I'll collect. Seriously, brother, an angry spirit isn't just a danger to Ashley, it's also a danger to you. In the same jewelry box, under the lining on the right side, is a small, silver letter opener. It has a cross on the top inlaid with mother of pearl. It's also been dipped in holy water and blessed by a priest. Be careful, Richard. I love you, brother."

"Love you too, sis, and thanks."

"Ashley, come in, come in. The cook is almost done. We're having salmon. I know it's one of your dad's favorites. Richard isn't here yet. He called and said he'd be few minutes late."

Ashley laughed. "Hello, Ann. It's good to see you."

Morgan walked up. "Is she chattering away again? Hello, Ashley. I'm glad we can help you and Richard with this little get-together. Take your coat off. What would you like to drink?"

"I'll have a margarita. Did Richard say how late he would be?"

"No, but he knows how important this is. I'm sure he'll get here soon."

Ashley had just settled down on the sofa with her margarita when the doorbell rang. She tensed in her seat. Ann answered the door, and Richard stood there.

Ashley's heart beat a little louder.

Morgan came up immediately. "Richard, I was afraid you had a problem with the slick roads."

"They are nasty, but I went slowly. No, the reason I'm late is I had to get a present for Ashley."

She got up from the couch. "You didn't need to get me a present."

He went to her and gave her a kiss. "Yes, I did. I'm glad you're wearing the blue dress."

He reached into his pocket and pulled out a small velvet box. "For you, so your parents can see that I'm serious." He handed her the box.

She opened it and stared. Inside was a beautiful dragonfly necklace. A row of small sapphires covered the body, with silver filigree wings spreading out on either side.

"Richard, I...I don't know what to say."

"Say you like it, and you'll wear it."

"I love it, and of course I will."

"Then allow me." He took the necklace out of the box and fastened it around her neck.

He stepped around her and nodded in admiration. "It looks good on you." He kissed her again.

The doorbell rang, and this time it was her parents.

After the introductions, everyone sat down at the table.

Morgan started the meal by passing the salmon, and general conversation started up.

"Everett, I understand you really liked Hawaii." Morgan put some asparagus spears on his plate.

Norma answered the question. "We loved it. The condo was right on the beach. All we had to do was walk out the door and straight into the ocean. We took several of the island tours. And the food, my goodness, I think I gained five pounds."

Ashley could feel her father's critical gaze as she concentrated on her plate.

Everett frowned and glanced at Richard. "Fowler, why is that name so familiar?"

Morgan grinned. "Because he's Jack Fowler's son."

Everett raised an eyebrow. "Really, Jack Fowler was your dad?"

"Yes, sir, at least that's what my mom said."

Ashley nearly choked on her drink.

Everett stared at him for a moment, then burst out laughing. "You're Jack's son, all right. The man would probably joke on his deathbed."

"He did, actually. He kept asking the nurses if they could hang an IV bag of bourbon on the pole." Richard took a bite of his dinner roll.

"I was sorry to hear he had passed away. I heard it was cancer." Everett picked up his glass of wine.

"Yes, he was a two-pack-a-day smoker, had been since was a teenager. Lung cancer got him in the end."

Morgan shook his head. "He was the best partner I ever had, fun to work with and a great head for business."

Richard smiled. "Thanks, Morgan." He picked up his wine glass in a salute.

Norma frowned. "Ashley, where did you get that necklace? It's absolutely beautiful."

She smiled. "Richard gave it to me just before you arrived." She turned and smiled at him.

"That looks like a valuable piece of antique jewelry." Norma stared at it.

Richard smiled. "It belonged to my grandmother. She had a real eye for lovely jewelry."

Ashley could practically see the gears moving behind her father's eyes. Expensive jewelry, the son of a developer and banker, her dad was calculating how wealthy Richard was. She glanced at Richard and caught his eye. He had noticed her father as well.

"What do you do for a living, Richard?" Everett took another sip of his wine.

"I'm a representative in the Idaho legislature, I run a sports bar, and I manage the family trust."

Everett smiled. "You sound like a very busy young man."

Ashley wanted to roll her eyes. At least Richard had passed the test. He had his own kingdom, and he could afford a princess.

Chapter 28
Chess Pieces

John paced his grave. Snow fell around him and through him, an unfriendly reminder that he could no longer walk the earth at will. Being stuck here for days frustrated him and chafed at his soul. He still couldn't figure out what had happened with Ashley. He lifted his hand; the burn marks on his fingers had faded, but the memory of the pain was still fresh. Why couldn't he touch her? He'd done it before; what stopped him this time? There were answers to his questions, but he'd need to go to Abaddon to get them, and dealing with the demon froze his very soul.

Abaddon had never said anything, but he was sure the demon knew he'd conserved his energy to dream-walk without authorization, and now he was being punished for it. Abaddon was holding him prisoner on his own burial plot. As degrading as that was, it was far better than the punishment he'd expected if he was caught.

A shiver ran down his spine, and he felt the demon's presence rather than saw it, that cold, hollow feeling of nothing. The raspy voice sounded in his mind.

"My need for you is coming to an end."

"Does that mean you'll release me, and I can live again?"

Abaddon appeared before him. "I will give you one last chance. I need you to distract Stephen Winship." He slowly walked around the plot.

"The best way to do this is to abduct either Ashley or Rose and bring the woman here."

John frowned. "I don't understand. What's so important about Winship?"

Abaddon stopped. "He is of no consequence. I simply do not want him to be governor."

John grinned. "It will be my pleasure to help with that."

"Good. You will find both women at home. Now go. You have only this night to succeed or fail." Abaddon disappeared.

John felt energy flow into his spirit, a lot of energy, more than he had ever had before. He smiled. That must have been the problem with Ashley; he'd had enough power to dream-walk but not enough to really control it. He closed his eyes and concentrated on Ashley's apartment.

Abaddon shook his head. "Such an arrogant fool, thinking it was only a lack of energy that stopped him. He doesn't understand that he is only a pawn in a greater game. Gabriel is trying to protect his pieces. The small barrier in the woman's mind would not have kept me out, but a lesser spirit would be burned." He rested his hand on the headstone. "It is only a matter of time before he is returned here for good. He simply needs to keep Gabriel distracted for a little while. A pawn sacrificed to hide the capture of a more important piece."

Ashley hung her coat in the closet and went over to the couch to take off her boots. She leaned back and took a deep breath. Tonight's dinner had gone far better than expected. Her father might not be completely sold on Richard, but he seemed pleased that she was dating him. Speaking of dates, tomorrow would be their first official one, dinner and *Phantom of The Opera*. Her green cocktail dress should be perfect for the occasion. She unzipped her boots and stretched her legs. Better get ready for bed; her first committee meeting was at eight.

Richard pulled up in his driveway just as his cell phone rang. "Hey, sis."

"Richard, are you with Ashley?"

"No. She should be home by now. We just had dinner at Morgan Tate's house with her parents. Why?"

"Did you give her the necklace?"

"Yes, just before the dinner."

"Hmm. Something is wrong. I've been reading the cards to see if I can tell what is happening with Ashley, and the reading keeps showing she's in danger. But you say you've given her the necklace."

"Liz, will you speak plainly, please." He parked the car in front of the door.

"Richard, I think she's in trouble. I have a real bad feeling. I think you need to go to her."

"Liz, it's snowing, and we have early committee meetings tomorrow." He turned off his car.

"Richard, I can't explain it in a way that will make you understand or believe. But please, brother, listen to me. You need to go to her, now. Trust me."

He narrowed his eyes. "Liz…"

"When you looked for the necklace, did you find the letter opener too?"

"Yes." This was beginning to make him uncomfortable."

"Take it with you. Go Richard, go now."

The line went dead.

If she's sending me out on a wild goose chase, I'm never going to forgive her. He started the car and put it into gear.

"Rose, I'm sorry I forgot to stop by the store on the way home. I got so tied up in the meeting with Mandy and the plans for the fundraiser that I completely forgot." Stephen grabbed two plates from the cupboard.

"I don't need anything for tonight's dinner, but I don't have anything in the house to make breakfast with tomorrow." She set glasses and silverware down on the table.

"Well, when we've finished with dinner, I can drive you to the store." He walked over to the table and set the plates down.

"Would you mind very much if I stayed home? I have some beads I need to stitch to a wedding dress this evening. The bride is coming in early tomorrow for a fitting, and I want to have it finished."

He stepped up to her and slid his arms around her waist. "For you, anything my dear." He bent down and kissed her.

Ashley tied the sash on her bathrobe and walked into the bathroom. She mentally listed the items on the agenda for her morning while she brushed her teeth. There were two bills she needed to read before going to bed to be prepared. She sighed and placed the toothbrush back in its holder. There always seemed to be one more thing to do before she could go to bed.

She walked into the living room and grabbed her briefcase. She set it on the dining table and headed to the kitchen to get a glass of water. A few minutes later, she was deep in concentration on a bill and making notes in the margins.

The doorknob turned so slowly that she barely noticed the sound. She looked up from her papers in time to see John step into her apartment.

She jumped up from her chair, bumping the table and knocking over the water glass.

"What do you think you're doing? Get out. You have no right to be here."

He left the door open and slowly walked toward her, a smirk on his face.

"Now, Ashley, is that anyway to treat a good friend?"

She moved and placed the table between them. "You are not a good friend. I barely know you. Now get out before I call the police." She stuck her hand in the pocket of her robe, hoping he'd think she had her cell phone with her, cursing herself for leaving it on the nightstand. She needed a weapon, but her Taser was in her purse and that sat in the bedroom as well. There were knives in the kitchen, but she didn't want to get that close to him.

He came up to the other side of the table. As he moved to one side, she moved to the other. "Oh, so that's it; you want to dance again. Well, come here, and I'll oblige you."

"Get out of my house." She mustn't panic. Whatever he was trying to do, she had to keep a level head and try to talk him out of it. "If you leave here now, I won't tell Bartlett what you've done, and you won't lose your job."

"Do you honestly think such a pitiful threat is going to stop me? I'm done with Bartlett. Come over here; I want to take you somewhere."

"I'm not going anywhere with you."

"Oh, yes you are."

He leapt around the table, and she tried to run for the door. He was too fast and knocked her to the floor. She tried to get up, but he grabbed her around the neck. She screamed, and he let her go. She crawled away.

John stood, shaking his arm and cursing. He held it out, and there was a perfect imprint of Ashley's dragonfly necklace burned into his skin.

"What is this?" He pointed to the burn.

Richard ran into the room and quickly assessed what had happened. "Ashley, get behind me. Did he hurt you?"

Ashley backed away. "No. I don't know how he got in here. I had the door locked."

John looked Richard up and down. "You can't save her. You don't know who you're dealing with."

Richard held out the letter opener and showed it to him. It didn't look very impressive, even though it did have a sharp point. "Actually, I do."

John looked at him, narrowed his eyes, and rushed forward.

Richard got his arm up in time and drove the silver point into John's shoulder. John screamed and tried to pull it out. He screamed even louder as it burned his hand. A moment later, he vanished, and the letter opener landed on the carpet.

Richard ran to the door, and he closed and locked it. He turned to see Ashley leaning against the wall, shaking, with all the color drained from her face. He walked over to her and gathered her in his arms. "It's all right. He's gone. I don't think he'll be back."

He held her close and kissed her forehead. "It's okay. I'm here."

She clung to him and cried on his shoulder. He stroked her hair and tried to soothe her. After a while, he could feel her shoulders relax.

She sniffed and rubbed her nose on her sleeve. "What is he?"

"That's a long story. Sit down on the couch while I get us both a drink and then I'll explain it to you."

Rose sat in a recliner, sewing beads along the shoulder of a wedding dress. The light of the floor lamp next to her illuminated her work. Four more beads and the pattern on this side of the dress would be complete. She shifted her position in the chair. Electric lights were so much better than the candles from her time. She'd never be able to do this kind of work without good light. A noise at the front door made her look up. She set down her sewing, thinking it was Stephen with an arm full of groceries. She got up and took a step toward the door and then froze. John stood in her living room.

"Well, well, my little wife," he snarled.

The look of hatred and anger in his face made her heart stop.

"You think you can leave me and run off with another man?" He took a step toward her.

She took a step backward. "I'm not your wife." She took another step back. She couldn't let him touch her. She couldn't let him hurt her child.

He scoffed. "You were mine first, and I don't share my things." He took another step.

She silently prayed. *Gabriel, help me. You promised to protect me.* She stepped back and bumped into the railing of the staircase.

"Come here, wife. We are going on a little trip." He took another step forward.

She felt the presence even before she saw the light. With the sound of soft footsteps and the rustling of cloth in a breeze, the archangel descended the stairs behind her. She closed her eyes and said a prayer of thanks. She opened them and saw the look of horror on John's face. The light engulfed him, and he started to scream. Pinpricks of light dotted his entire body and grew larger. John kept screaming, a truly horrible sound. The light continued to spread until his entire body was engulfed in it.

Rose shook as the light consumed him before her eyes. A few minutes later, John was gone.

Gabriel's voice sounded in her mind. "You're safe now, Rose. You won't see him again. He…" The angel stopped speaking, and the light grew dimmer.

"So, that's what he was up to. Sacrifice a pawn to take a castle." The light grew even dimmer.

"Stephen will be here soon. Tell him what happened, and that John is gone for good. I will see you again." The light disappeared.

Frank's fingers shook as he punched the numbers on his cell phone. Marion picked up on the third ring.

"Are you watching television?" he asked.

"No, I was reading a book. Why?"

"Turn on your television, channel seven and hurry." Frank could hear the sound of Marion walking on a hardwood floor. An electronic crackle and then the voice of the news reporter:

"The story has been confirmed by Mason Radnor, the late governor's chief of staff. Governor Bartlett had been seeing a doctor, and there was talk of possible surgery, but no one expected this. For those of you who are just joining our broadcast, Idaho Governor Russell James Bartlett died this evening of an apparent heart attack. Lieutenant Governor Michael Hampton was sworn in as the new governor a few minutes ago by Curtis Patterson, chief justice of the Idaho Supreme Court. State flags will be flying at half-mast for the next few days, and we will be reporting on the funeral arrangements as soon as they are made public. Governor Russell Bartlett, dead at the age of sixty-seven."

Marion's voice sounded choked. "Do Stephen and Richard know?"

"I tried to call them, but neither one is answering the phone."

"Frank, what does this mean?"

"It means everything is about to change."

Other Titles Available
From Augustina Van Hoven

The Rose series

The Kiss of a Rose

The Bloom of a Rose

Love through Time series

A Second Chance

The Kiss of a Rose
Excerpt: Chapter 1

I must be out of my mind.

Stephen Winship covered his eyes as the wind whipped up another flurry of snow around his face. This was becoming ridiculous. He could see only a few feet in front of him as he trudged through the cemetery. It didn't matter, though. He'd made a promise, and it wasn't conditional on convenience or good weather.

The tops of old grave markers guided him like stone sentinels through the trees and bushes in the oldest part of the graveyard. The foliage was thick and overgrown. Ominous. A shiver ran down his spine. He squeezed his way around a particularly large evergreen that partially blocked his path—then froze.

In front of him stood the statue of a woman, the most beautiful woman he had ever seen. She wore a gown loosely gathered at her waist, its voluminous folds floating out nearly to the ground. Her long hair flowed down the sides of her face and spilled over her back in finely sculpted waves and curls. She gazed at a large bouquet of flowers she held in her delicate hands. The sad look in her eyes caused him to take a step closer.

She had wings that were slightly opened, giving the illusion she would soon take flight. Stephen stared at her, captivated. Around him the wind subsided, and only a few light snowflakes fell.

An artist, sculpting white marble with reverence and love, had fashioned this beauty with amazing perfection. It looked as though he had taken a heavenly angel and turned her into stone.

Stephen removed his glove, reached into the bouquet of mixed flowers he carried, and pulled out a single red rose. He laid it with great care at her feet.

The bright red petals barely touched the base of the statue; the leaves and long stem spread out over the snow. With one last look, he turned and walked away, reluctantly leaving her in the sanctuary of evergreens.

Continuing along the path of old gravestones, Stephen was relieved to find two wooden posts marking the way to the main road that wound through the large cemetery. Turning left, he followed the road to where the more recent burials had taken place and began searching.

Stephen scraped the snow away from a small tombstone marked "Margaret Winship." Digging a little deeper, he revealed a date of death four months earlier, August 5. He carefully spread the bouquet of flowers he carried out over the snow. The colors glowed as they lay on the newly fallen blanket.

"Happy Birthday, Mom. I promised you flowers, and here they are." He coughed to clear his throat. "You probably don't even recognize me under all these clothes. This is the coldest and snowiest December I've ever seen. I can't stay long. The car's stuck in a drift, and there's more snow on the way. I'll be back when the weather is better." He heard his monologue and realized he had nothing more to say. She would understand. She always had. He kissed his fingers and touched them to the etched surface of her name.

"I miss you, Mom."

Taking one last look at the cold, wet headstone, he turned and retraced his steps.

His path led him back to the shelter of the pines that protected the marble angel. The beauty of her sculpted face captured him as it had before. His eyes followed the flowing folds of her gown until they ended at the base of the pedestal. He blinked in surprise. The rose he had placed there was nowhere to be found. He looked around to see if it had perhaps been blown away by the wind. There were no footprints other than his own, not even from an animal. Only an imprint of the rose remained. Stephen blinked and shivered. He checked again to see if he had missed a clue, but there was no trace of his gift.

Stephen trudged back to his car in silence. He unlocked the doors, pulled a shovel from the back, and started digging to free the tires from the snowdrift. Forty-five minutes later, tired and sweaty, he drove his car along the still-deserted streets. Heavy snowflakes fell, and his windshield wipers barely kept up. The heater blew the cold winter air over the windows while the engine warmed up. A strange smell came from the vents. Stephen inhaled deeply.

The scent of roses hung in the air like an enticing perfume.

The Bloom of a Rose

Excerpt: Chapter 1

The battle on the chessboard is a game of war with each side attempting to capture the opposing king. When the players are equally matched, the conflict comes down to sheer determination and the willingness to sacrifice.

The angel Gabriel stood beside a large oak tree, watching the proceedings. Prominent citizens and government officials had assembled once again at Morris Hill Cemetery to bury one of their own. Surrounded by his friends and enemies, the body of the late governor, Russell Bartlett, waited to be lowered into its final resting place.

Gabriel sighed. Why was it that men were always kind and respectful of one another when it was too late to ask forgiveness?

Gabriel changed his position. It was best not to linger. Abaddon, his demon opponent, could arrive at any moment. This situation was Abaddon's temporary victory. The game wasn't over. He scanned the crowd. Most of his chess pieces were here at this funeral and a few of Abaddon's as well. There was still time to stop the demon's plan, but it was running short. His next move would have to be made tonight.

Rachel held the handkerchief against her face, trying in vain to stem the flow of tears. She stood beside her mother and listened to the minister conduct the graveside funeral service. A large crowd had gathered to pay their respects to the late governor of Idaho, but she stood alone, mourning a father who the others would never know.

Only last week, they had had breakfast together in his office. How could he possibly be gone? In a few years, he was supposed to walk her down the aisle on her wedding day. Now it would be some friend of the family. He would never see her graduate from college or bounce his grandchild on his knee. She wiped her eyes again, knowing that the large hole in her heart would never be filled.

A huge spray of white and yellow roses adorned the coffin, but all she could see was his body lying on the floor of the bedroom where he had fallen. The doctors had said he had suffered a massive heart attack. She sniffed and wiped her nose.

Her mother moved beside her, moving her weight from one foot to the other. Sarah Bartlett was a small woman, barely five feet tall. Her silver hair and pleasant face gave her a friendly, grandmotherly appearance, until you looked into her cold gray eyes. A reporter once described her as a soft outer shell covering a frame of steel. Today, the steel showed through as she stood stone-faced, staring at the coffin.

The service was coming to an end, and soon some of the other attendees would shake her hand, giving her their condolences. Rachel wanted to turn and run as far away as possible. The only thing that kept her feet rooted to the spot was the knowledge that her father would want her to show courage, despite her sorrow.

The minister began the closing prayer; she wiped her face and took a deep breath.

Paul Miller stood between his two friends, Stephen Winship with his wife Rose, and Richard Fowler with his girlfriend, Senator Ashley Halliday. Paul glanced around at the other attendees and wondered what he was doing in such esteemed company. He'd been a member of the Idaho legislature for less than a month. A chill ran down his spine; he reached up and adjusted his scarf against the cold. It was early February, the air was crisp, and there were still patches of snow on the ground.

Three years ago, he had buried his own father on a morning much like this. The memory weighed heavy on his heart. He looked over at the governor's family and saw Rachel wipe her eyes. He knew that pain. It had lightened over time, but the core of it still remained. He wanted to tell her that, but this was not the time or the place. Besides, he'd only met her once, and she would probably not welcome his comments.

He bit his lip. It was likely that he would know that pain again … and soon. He flexed his fingers inside his gloves. The doctor had diagnosed his mother with a heart condition only the week before. He'd been living in her home since the legislature went into session. It was a shorter commute in winter weather, and his mother wanted the company. She constantly complained about being tired, and he found her sleeping in a chair every time he came home. It took a while to persuade her to go to her doctor, but she finally went.

The fear of losing another parent ran through his veins like ice water. Although it is a situation that every child someday faces, no matter how old you are, you are never really prepared for it.

Paul glanced behind himself. He had the uncomfortable feeling that eyes were boring into his back. He shifted his weight. The service was coming to an end, and he needed to pay attention. He straightened his shoulders. After the service, he would walk over to his father's grave and pay his respects.

Stephen slipped his arm around his wife, Rose. "I need to get Rose out of the cold."

Richard leaned around Paul. "Why don't we all head over to my bar. I could do with a good drink, and we definitely need to talk."

Stephen looked around. "Let's go before we draw attention to ourselves. Are you coming too, Paul?"

"I have to run a quick errand, but I will meet you there."

Richard held out his hand. "Come on, Ashley. I want to get out of here before the traffic is too backed up."

Both couples disappeared into the crowd.

Paul glanced over at Rachel. She stood next to her mother, wiping her tears as mourners came up to offer condolences. Even in the depth of her grief she still had poise and grace. The breeze blew her long, brown hair over her face hiding the cupid bow lips he found so appealing. He wanted to go over there and rescue her, but there really wasn't anything he could do. It was time to slip away and head for his father's grave. Richard was right. The traffic would be snarled as everyone tried to leave the cemetery. He'd parked out on a side street, and with a little luck, he could avoid the worst of the gridlock.

He made his way through the large cemetery, following the main road past the older section to his father's burial site. The wind whipped up and blew his hair into his face. He put up a hand to shield his eyes. A small rounded headstone with the image of an angel carved above the name was in front of him. He rubbed his face and read the worn writing: "Molly Margaret O'Brien, Born 1861 – Died 1914." He reached out to the stone and used it to help balance himself until the wind subsided. A dog barked in the distance, and he straightened; it was time to hurry if he wanted to meet the others at the bar.

His father's grave was in the newer section of the cemetery, not far from Stephen's mother. Paul stuck his hands in his pockets and bowed his head against the now steadily blowing wind. He wouldn't stay long, just the few minutes it took to tell his father about the last few weeks. He'd last visited the grave a few days before Christmas and wanted to tell his dad about the new legislative session. It took him another five minutes to reach his destination. The wind was getting worse. A storm was coming, and it would bring snow or sleet when it arrived. He wanted to be indoors somewhere by that time.

Thomas Miller's grave lay next to a large oak tree. During the fall, acorns and leaves covered the ground, but at this time of year, only brown grass covered the surface. Unlike the other graves around it, this one had no snow. The branches of the tree protected it, even though they were bare. The roots of the large tree were slowly lifting the soil so the headstone had a slight tilt.

Paul stood at the foot of his father's final resting place and stared at the stone. Cancer. His father had been a pack a day smoker since he was sixteen. Neither Paul nor his brother, Sam, had ever picked up the habit. They'd both seen what it had done to their dad.

He rubbed his shoulders. It was getting colder. Best say what he planned to say and head for the car. Where to begin? "Hello, Dad. It's been a while since I came to visit…"

Paul spoke for a while as his breath steamed and blew away with each gust of wind. He was close to the end when the sound of running feet drew his attention to the road. He glanced around the tree and froze. Rachel was running toward him.

He stepped out from behind the tree just in time for her to run into him.

The impact nearly knocked him to the ground. He held onto her to keep his balance, and she screamed.

"It's okay. Rachel, it's okay. I'm not going to hurt you. Rachel. Rachel?" He shook her, and she lifted her head, revealing her tear-stained face. He could see in her eyes that she didn't recognize him. "Rachel, I'm Representative Paul Miller. We met last month at the Governor's Ball."

She looked at his face for a moment, then buried her head in his chest and cried. He wrapped his arms around her and let her grieve.

After a while, her shoulders relaxed and only a few sobs escaped her lips. She slowly moved away from him and stood with her head lifted up to face him.

"I'm sorry."

"Don't apologize. I know what you're going through. I've been there myself." Paul reached into his coat and pulled out a handkerchief. He handed it to her. She nodded her head and dabbed her eyes.

"Thank you, Mr. Miller."

"Please, call me Paul." A gust of wind blew his hair back. "The storm is almost here. Is your car nearby?"

She blew her nose. "No, it's on the other side of the cemetery." She frowned. "What are you doing in this part of the graveyard?"

"Paying my respects to my father before I leave." He motioned to the headstones behind him.

"I'm sorry." She sniffed. "When did it happen?"

"Almost three years ago."

She looked at his handkerchief. "Thank you. I'll have it laundered and get it back to you. I'm afraid it's rather wet."

"It's going to get a whole lot wetter if we don't get under cover soon. The storm is about to break. My car is just over there. If you'll come with me, I can drive you over to yours or take you home, if you'd rather do that."

"Thank you. If you could take me to my car, that would be great." She wiped her eyes again.

"Sure, this way."

He led her quickly along the road. The first drops of sleet were falling when they reached his SUV. He opened the door for her, then ran around the vehicle and slipped into the driver's seat while the drops fell faster as they rode through the cemetery, he was grateful that he'd bought the deluxe version of this model SUV. The built-in seat warmers were coming in very handy while the engine warmed up.

Rachel really was parked on the other side of the cemetery. The mourners who had been at the governor's funeral had all cleared out, and her car stood parked on the side of the road all alone.

She fished her keys out of her pocket as he pulled up next to her vehicle.

"Thank you, Paul, for the ride, the handkerchief, and . . ." She stopped speaking.

He reached out and touched her hand. "Rachel, the pain of your loss will never go away, but over time, you will find that it is easier to live with." He reached into his pocket and pulled out a business card. "If you ever need someone to talk to, call me. I'm a good listener."

She took the card. "Thank you," she said as she slid out of the car and stepped over to hers.

He waited until she got it started, then waved and drove away, wondering if he'd ever hear from her again.

ABOUT THE AUTHOR

Augustina Van Hoven was born in The Netherlands and currently resides in the Pacific Northwest with her husband, two dogs, and three cats. She is an avid reader of romance, science fiction and fantasy. When she's not writing, she likes to work in her garden or, in the winter months, crocheting or knitting on her knitting machines.

Look for more intriguing romances from Augustina, who is hard at work on two new series:

* *A Second Chance*, a time-travel romance that's part of her Love Through Time series, is coming out in the Fall of 2017.

* *The Last Christmas on Earth*, a prequel to her futuristic romance series called A New Frontier, is also coming out in the Fall of 2017. The first book in that series is due in Spring 2018.